It's not a dead end if it takes you
somewhere you needed to go.

UNCONDITIONAL

A NOVEL

EVA MARIE EVERSON

BASED ON THE MOTION PICTURE SCREENPLAY BY

BRENT McCORKLE

978-1-4336-7946-9

Published by B&H Publishing Group
Nashville, Tennessee

Exclusive representation by
Working Title Agency, LLC, Spring Hill, Tennessee

Dewey Decimal Classification: F
Subject Heading: INTERPERSONAL RELATIONS—FICTION \ LOVE
STORIES \ DESPAIR—FICTION

1 2 3 4 5 6 7 8 • 16 15 14 13 12

to Jordynn

". . . more than blueberry pie."

"Let the little children come to me, and do not hinder them, for the kingdom of heaven belongs to such as these."

MATTHEW 19:14

Chapter One

LIFE USED TO be so beautiful. So full of magic and possibilities. Wonder and excitement. There wasn't anything I couldn't do. Couldn't be. Couldn't go.

When I was a child, I would sit for hours drawing and dreaming up crazy stories to tell all my friends. Multicolored crayon tales etched by wild imaginings. Stories about a place where the sun always shone. Or a place where a tin man could carry a little red-headed girl to the farthest point of the universe, way above the earth, on feet made of fire. Or a lonely island way out in the middle of the ocean, where a deer and a platypus lived in disharmony. They sat back-to-back on this tiny piece of land, never acknowledging each other. Until one day when they were both thirsty, the deer climbed up a coconut tree so they could share a drink. After that, they were the best of friends.

I thought my stories would inspire the world, make it a better place somehow. I was such a dreamer. And for a while it seemed that all my dreams would come true.

Billy Crawford was my world. The man of my dreams. The man I promised to love and honor and cherish until "death do us part." Believing, of course, that death would never really come.

Or that if it did, it would be a long way off in the future. Too far away to worry about today. Or even tomorrow.

Billy worked for the power company. I used to brag, "Wherever it's dark, Billy brings light."

Billy would laugh and say, "But only if there's a switch to flip."

While Billy made the world brighter, I wrote children's books, letting all who would read them know that the fairy tale did exist. Everyone and anyone could have all they wanted and more. All they had to do was believe in their dreams.

But how quickly dreams can be shattered. In one second. With one gun. One bullet cracking the silence of one night.

A dragon had come to slay my knight.

But that killer didn't just take Billy's life. He took mine too. Like Rapunzel, he locked me in a cold, dark tower where I lived alone, unable to climb down to where the world was green and warmed by sunshine. Colors had faded to black and white. The places that—once upon a time—had freely been mine were now barred to me.

WHEN IT CAME to Billy's murder, the only thing the police knew was that the killer wore a red hoodie and left behind a red mechanic's rag. They investigated for a few days. Maybe even weeks, if I think about it. They asked questions of all the wrong kinds of people. And then, without a single lead, they gave up their search. They placed Billy's file under the heading of "cold case" and also started investigating the next homicide, which they probably never solved.

But I could never move on.

Instead, I spent hours in my tower, drawing a new kind of story. Shadows of a man dressed in red. Tales of an oily, filthy rag, dropped like some kind of claimer's stake, marking off the deed. I drew those pictures and kept them tacked over my desk in the hayloft of our barn—mine and Billy's. And while the police moved on to other things, I stared at my dark art, determined to make a new kind of difference.

After a while, as prisoners will sometimes do, I grew to love my place in the tower, to relish the hours in the dark, studying those drawings. I found myself not minding the bitterness. Instead, I was somehow unexplainably existing on my sheer determination to right this horrible wrong. Those hours and those drawings kept me close to Billy, close to the final minutes of his life. Without them, nothing that was left to me made sense.

What do you do when you've lost your faith? Your hope? Your will to go on? What do you do when life doesn't make sense anymore? When drawing a breath—a single breath—takes all your effort, until even the effort is gone?

I used to dream of telling stories.

But I never dreamed mine would end like this.

Chapter Two

THE WEEK BEFORE Billy died, I stood by the living room window of our farmhouse, staring past the lawn, the maples, and the split-rail fence to the ribbon of dirt road I knew he'd be driving down any minute. I held my sketchbook in one hand, the edge of the curtain in the other. Anticipating. Watching. Giggling like a schoolgirl.

I could hear his truck before I could see it. That blue-and-white '66 Ford Custom Cab—the very same one he'd picked me up in for our first date—belched out enough fumes and noise to wake the dead. After a few months of dating, when I asked him why he'd chosen to pick me up in such a relic, he said he figured if I was cool enough to go out with him in that old pickup, then I was worth keeping. Just like she was.

That day—that magical day the week before he died, before I knew how precious little time we had left—I stood at the window, listening. The truck barreled down the road doing about thirty-five miles an hour, which was ten miles over what it should have been driven. As soon as it passed through the gate, I dropped the curtain and dashed over to the living room's blue-green velvet sofa, planting myself so it'd appear I'd been sitting there for hours, drawing the title page for my next best seller. Like time had been lost to me.

I suppressed a giggle as the driver's door creaked open and slammed shut. I kept drawing as Billy's boots shuffled up the wooden steps of our cypress-log cabin, to the stained porch, and finally to one of the ten-paneled glass French doors. The door opened with a squeak and closed with a rattle.

"Hey, cowboy," I said without looking up.

"Hey, purty lady," he said, sounding more like he'd just woken up than gotten home from work. "You make it to the bank for me today?"

"I did."

"Good, 'cuz I just ran out." Billy stepped around the back of the sofa, leaned over, and kissed the top of my head. I drew in a breath—he smelled of warm sunshine and that morning's aftershave.

I cut my eyes over to his, all crystal blue and focused on mine. After a moment he sat beside me, dropping his gaze to my lap. "And you are finally gonna write that thing. *Firebird*. Betcha it'll be your best ever."

His eyes returned to my face, and for a moment we were locked in our own kind of embrace. We didn't need our arms or hands or even the words people who are in love say to each other. We had our eyes, and that was enough.

"All right. So where they at?" He kissed my cheek, stood, and walked back toward the door.

"What? Where's what at?"

"My two-dollar bills. My Jeffersons?" He stopped at the old ladder on the wall, the one he'd stained and added some hooks to and positioned between two windows framed by knotty pine. He hooked his white hard hat on one, his work jacket on another.

"Oh," I said, returning to my drawing, all the while pretending it was my sole focus in life. "I put them in the coffee mug cabinet."

"The coffee mug cabinet?"

I kept my head down, but my eyes followed him toward the kitchen.

"Now why in the world would you want to go and do that?"

He opened the cabinet and hit the floor in one fluid movement. Three carefully placed hens flew out, clucking and carrying on. And why shouldn't they? They'd been kept in there long enough, waiting for his return.

I dropped my sketch pad to the floor. Billy hauled himself up, brow cocked, looking more boy than man. "Oh, you're gonna get it," he said.

I was out of the door in a flash, dashing across the porch, jumping down the stairs. I ran as fast as I could, with half of my long red hair flying behind me, the other half slapping me in the face.

Billy gained on me in the barn where he tackled me, and tossed me into a pile of hay. Dust and broken pieces of grain swirled around us. He held me there for a few moments, tickling me until I had nothing left but gasps and giggles.

"Come on," he said when he knew he'd worn me out. "Let's take the horses out for a ride."

We rode for what could have been hours but felt more like minutes. We cantered through the fields of our property, staying close to the tree line, past rolled bales of hay, and up to a summit where the air had grown thick with evening and the sky had turned to fire. Still sitting astride our saddles, we watched the sun set, waited for the afterglow, neither of us saying a word. We didn't need to. Billy and I could read each other without speaking.

Finally, he said, "I love you, you know that?"

I nodded. "I love you too, cowboy."

And I did. More than anything in this life, I did.

THAT SATURDAY MORNING Billy came up with the idea of going camping.

"Camping? Tonight?"

"Why not?" He'd just come out of the shower, towel wrapped around his waist, water trickling down his chest. His hair stood on end in wet spikes of adorable. "The weather's perfect for it. We can ride Cricket and Penny out to the west side of the property. Watch the sun go down. Build a fire . . ." He pretended to act sheepish. "You know . . . and fool around a little."

I laughed out loud.

He walked over to the bed where I sat propped up, sipping on coffee and reading a novel.

I closed the book, laid it on the bedside table next to my coffee mug, and reached for the white chenille comforter to draw it over and around him as he climbed in next to me. "It's been a long time since we went camping," I said.

"I know." His left index finger ran the length of my bare arm, drawing gooseflesh.

"I don't even remember how long."

"Too long."

"I think the pup tent's in the barn somewhere."

"I'll get it." His eyes met mine. "You can bring your sketch book. Keep working on that story."

"Firebird."

"Mm-hmm." By now his lips traced where his finger had drawn. "So . . . what do you say?"

"What do I say?" I asked, sliding under the cover, drawing it tight under my chin. "I think camping is a fine idea."

To which Billy fell back onto his side of the bed and laughed.

THE NIGHT TURNED magical. Billy dug a pit, surrounding it with rocks, and made a fire, while I threw our sleeping bags and camping pillows between it and the tent. The fall air was crisp, and the fire warmed us, singing a crackling tune, joining voices with the crickets and the occasional tenor hoot owl. Earlier we'd watched as the sun slipped behind the hills, bathing them in an orangey glow until they grew black, forming only an outline against a midnight-blue sky. Now I sat cross-legged with my sketch pad in my lap, colored pencils between my teeth and behind my ears, working furiously on my little firebird. Billy poked the fire awhile before leaning back on his elbow and staring upward. Knowing Billy, he was probably counting the stars and looking for those he could wish upon.

After a while I sensed him studying me, so I looked over at him and smiled.

"You finally started your book?" he asked.

I went back to my work. "No," I said around the pencil before removing it. "It's just an idea at this point. It's nowhere near where it needs to be."

"Tell it to me."

I tilted my chin toward him. Gave him "the eye." Billy was always teasing me about my stories. Saying things like, "All right for children, but I'm not sure you can make a film out of it." But the truth was, Billy was nothing if not proud of me.

"I'll be nice," he said, though his smile was crooked, making me doubt the sincerity of the words. But the firelight played across his face, bringing out his boyish charm. "C'mon."

"All right." I chose another of my colored pencils from behind my right ear, tucked the first one in its place, and went back to work. After a deep breath, I began with the words that had been forming in my head for such a long time. "Once upon a time, there lived a little baby oriole named Firebird. Now Firebird just lived for the sunshine. He would bask in that glow for hours and hours. But when the rains would come, he would complain to his mama. He wanted to know why God gave storms the power to take the sun away. And Mama bird would just smile and say, 'You'll understand someday, when you walk on the clouds.'"

Again, I pulled a pencil from behind my ear and replaced it with the one I'd been using. After a moment of careful sketching,

I returned to my story. "Now, over and over again, the rains would come. And over and over again, little Firebird would complain to his mama. But one day, when a huge storm rolled in, his mama had a different answer. 'It's up there waiting for you. But you have to go see it for yourself.'

"Now Firebird was scared. He hadn't used his wings much at all. Yet up he went into the great unknown."

I looked at my husband. His face was somber. His eyes intent.

"Danger," I said. "Turbulence."

Billy gave me a half smile. I watched the rise and fall of his chest. His breathing that told me that, like a child, he was right there in the moment of the story.

I looked at my sketch pad, to the wide-eyed oriole I had fashioned from colored pencils and imagination. "But instead of answers, he was met with lightning, thunder, and howling wind. He feared the storm would rip him apart. He was on the verge of turning back when . . ." I looked at Billy. ". . . it happened. He broke through the clouds. And there it was: The sun, more beautiful than ever. And in that moment, it all became clear. No storm could take the sun away. The sun was *always* shining."

I tore the page from the pad, slipped it toward Billy. "It was as constant as his mother's love. All he needed to see it was a little 'walk on the clouds.'"

Billy looked at my drawing and then back up to me. He was proud of me. Proud of my ability to tell my stories. Proud to call me his wife. As proud as I was to call him my husband.

I looked back at the fire. Watched it lick away at the night air.

"Not bad," Billy finally said. "For a start."

I felt my heart smile before it reached my face. "I should have known you'd say something like that."

Billy grinned. "I love it. Best one yet, didn't I tell you?"

"You keep that drawing for me, you hear?"

"I'll put it in my wallet. Carry it everywhere I go."

The flames popped.

"Sam, you gotta write this. Every story you write gets better, but this one is the best. Seriously. Write it. Promise me."

"All right," I said. "I promise."

THREE DAYS LATER the rains came. By the second day it seemed that somewhere out there a man named Noah ought to be building an ark. Late one afternoon, after putting in an already difficult day, Billy got called in to work, as we knew he would.

"Don't wait up," he said, tucking the white hard hat under his arm. "I'm probably gonna be awhile."

"I won't," I said. But I knew I would.

It was about ten o'clock when I received the call from the police officer over in Nashville telling me I needed to come down to a neighborhood known as the Commons, to a small grocery store called Murphy's. He said there had been an accident involving Billy, and he gave me the address.

"Is he all right?" I asked, already jumping into a pair of riding boots I kept by the front door.

"You just need to come on down. That's all I know to tell you right now, Mrs. Crawford."

I ran out of the door and into the pouring rain, not bothering with an umbrella. Once inside the car, I was soaked through and through, but I didn't care. My hands shook as I tried to start the car. I dropped the keys to the floorboard, had to retrieve them in the dark. When I finally got the car started, I jerked it into gear and bounced over the ruts in our driveway. I was doing close to forty-five by the time I drove through the gate.

Usually Nashville is a thirty-minute drive. That night it was more like an hour. An hour of shaking uncontrollably, in spite of the self-reassuring prayers I spoke aloud, telling God to make it all right. Once inside the city limits, I plugged my GPS navigator into the cigarette lighter and typed in the address while waiting at a red light. The system told me I was only five minutes away. Five minutes from knowing what I know now. Five minutes from my life never being the same again.

I saw the reflection of flashing red lights before anything else, each one running across the dark, rain-drenched buildings like mice scurrying from a cat. I parked the car as close as I could get, and then got out and ran toward the ambulance and police cars.

I remember now how my mind registered seeing the ambulance, thinking it was a good sign. If Billy were dead, I reasoned, there'd be no need for an ambulance. Its presence surely meant he was alive. Maybe he'd been shocked by a live wire. Or fallen off a ladder. He'd spend time in the hospital, but after a week or so he'd be back at home. Then back to work. Life would return to normal. Surely . . .

I reached the building where a dark-green awning with the words Murphy's Liquor Store hung over the door and the front stoop.

Bars were on the windows, painted black and slick with rain. Handmade signs pressed up against the glass from the inside were barely readable. But my mind, it grasped it all. Every word. Every advertisement. Even the graffiti spray-painted next to the front door.

I could see people standing in clusters, staring toward an alleyway, so I walked quickly toward them.

"Whoa there." A hand grabbed my shoulder.

I turned to face a police officer, who stared down at me. "I'm—I'm Samantha Crawford," I told him. "I got a call. Something about my husband?"

His face, young and red-cheeked, grew somber. He looked over my shoulder. "Oh, yes, ma'am. You need to come with me."

His hand slipped authoritatively around my forearm. He drew me along until we stood at the mouth of the alley, alongside several other officers, their breath visible in the cold night air. The rain was relentless, making it difficult to see. I wiped my hands across my eyes and focused on what lay ahead.

Yellow police tape sectioned off the scene. A female investigator, blonde hair pulled back in a ponytail, was kneeling under an umbrella and holding a camera. The flash went off, exposing the body of a man lying face up, half covered by a blanket.

"Billy!"

I started to run to my husband, but the officer who had led me there held me back.

"Wait up, ma'am. That's a crime scene. There's Detective Miller," he said, pointing to a middle-aged man with swept-back silver-gray hair. He wore only dress pants, a shirt, and a dark sports jacket, yet somehow appeared unaffected by the weather or the chaos around him. "He's in charge. You gotta wait here till he tells you something."

The shaking deep inside turned violent. A crime scene, the officer called it. This was more than a shock by a live wire or a fall from a ladder. The axis on which my world spun was being torn from its place. "That's . . . that's my *husband!*" I said, pointing.

"Here," the officer said, taking off his jacket and wrapping it around me. "Just wait right here. I'll see what I can find out for you."

I methodically slipped my arms into the oversized jacket as he went to talk with the detective. I took careful steps forward, cautious not to draw attention from the other officers. I wanted to be—*had* to be—close enough to hear what was happening. To see. But even from only a few yards away, I wasn't near enough to see Billy's face, to know if he were alive or dead.

Another man dressed much like Detective Miller joined the detective where Billy lay. They both squatted.

"What have we got?" I heard Miller shout over the rain.

"One shot to the chest. Large caliber." He pointed to the wall behind him. "Lodged back there." He pointed to where I stood with the other officers, the emergency medical responders, and the growing number of bystanders speaking in hushed tones. "Here's the strange part: I got three more shots down here."

"Witness reports?"

"Only that the shooter was wearing a red hoodie."

"Surprise, surprise," Miller said, standing again.

The officer who'd been with me stood to the side of the detectives, waiting. The three of them spoke for a moment before the officer turned and nodded in my direction. I watched Miller's head droop like a sad old dog's. His hands went to his hips, fingers splayed close to the metal badge hooked to his belt on one side, a holstered gun on the other. He took several steps toward me, walking with a slight limp. I focused on a single button of his white shirt beneath the dark blue jacket. I could see that the rain had plastered it to his barrel chest. He looked up and our eyes met, just as the second detective reached for the blanket and pulled it over Billy's face.

"No!"

My legs buckled, and my knees crashed against the asphalt.

I remember nothing else.

Chapter Three

One Year Later

THE LAST THING I wanted to do was attend a black-tie affair at the Opryland Hotel, where I was being honored for my "continued work toward children's literacy." I didn't want to deal with all that pressed white linen and crystal gleaming under massive, low-lit chandeliers. Or the scent of fine perfumes and men's cologne, rich aromatic coffee and chocolate desserts swirled with raspberry sauce. The crowd of people, dressed to the nines, sitting straight-backed on padded seats. The calling of my name, the walk to the stage, the standing at the podium where I'd be forced to give a speech I'd been working on for weeks.

I wanted nothing to do with any of it.

I'd gone through scads of paper trying to come up with something appropriate to say. Looking at the wadded discards overflowing my trash can, it was a wonder I'd ever made a dime as a writer. The words simply wouldn't come. I couldn't string ten of them together to form a coherent thought. Nothing about the award—which was for a book I'd written before Billy died and had been published about a month after—made sense. So I'd written a book and managed to give a few thousand of them away to the public schools. So what?

It wasn't like it had cost me anything much. Not like losing my husband. My life. My reason for breathing. I'd been so enmeshed in my misery, I'd hardly considered the impact of the gesture. Then I received a call from my agent telling me about the award banquet.

"You have to do this, Sam," Jonathan said, a few days before the event. "You *have* to get out, and this is as good a place as any to start."

"I can't," I told him. "Not yet."

"It's been a year, Sam. It's time."

"I don't know. I don't think I can."

"Do it, Sam. For me. For Billy."

Sending a simple "thank you" via my agent was not enough. And, as Jonathan had said, not going was out of the question.

He had given me an idea, though. Eventually I wrote the speech to focus more on Billy. As I placed the emphasis on my one true inspiration and the gifts *he'd* left behind, the words poured out of me and onto paper so easily. I was amazed I hadn't thought of it sooner.

At the banquet, after a dinner of steak, twice-baked potatoes, asparagus, and the chocolate cake with raspberry sauce I'd come to expect at such events, I pretended to listen as my publisher eloquently introduced me. When Shannon called my name, I rose amid the applause, lifted my black gown to just over my ankles, and climbed the steps to the stage.

I kept my focus on the podium until I reached it and then smiled out over the sea of faces who smiled back at me. Many of them I'd never seen before this night. Some of them I knew, of course. Some I knew well. Those were the ones who tilted their chins just enough to give me encouragement. It was the support I needed to even begin speaking.

I took a deep breath, unrolled the two-dollar bill I'd kept clutched in my hand since Shannon had begun her speech, and spread it out before me. Behind me, a large screen displayed the cover of my latest work. My *last* work.

Other than the speech I was about to give, I hadn't written a single word since Billy died.

I took a second breath, squared my shoulders. "What an honor it is to be here," I began. "I'm still not certain how a children's author receives such a prestigious award for giving away a few books."

I paused long enough to allow the polite laughter—a kind offering, I thought—to subside. "Everyone here seeks to make a difference in this world. My husband, Billy, would have been right at home with all of you. This evening I'd like to share Billy's idea about changing the world with *love*."

There was applause, and I was grateful—I needed another moment to compose myself. I tried to focus on the faces. Then just one face, Jonathan's, who sat in the seat next to my empty chair. But doing so became increasingly difficult. With a glance over my shoulder, I saw the image of my book on the screen had been replaced with a graphic of a two-dollar bill.

Did you get my Jeffersons?

"The two-dollar bill," I said, looking back at the audience. "It came to be Billy's symbol of love. You see, there are millions of these bills in print, more than enough to go around. But they are hardly ever seen. People hoard them, keep them hidden away. Billy would . . . he would always say, 'There's enough love to go around, Sam. You just have to share it.'"

I looked down at the podium, at the two-dollar bill that had seen better days. My fingertips hovered over it, quivering. "He . . . he got this crazy idea . . ." My head started to spin. "He began giving away two-dollar bills to total strangers. It was . . . it was his way . . . it was his way of . . ."

I could barely see past the tears shimmering between myself and the audience. People who, by the looks on their faces, could see my pain and knew it had become too much to bear. I looked down at the podium again, scooped the wrinkled bill into my hand. "I'm sorry," I said.

I crossed the stage as quickly as I could, stumbling blindly toward the stairs. A man's hand reached for mine. I took it, figuring it was probably Jonathan's. Not that it mattered. In that moment I would have grasped at anything. Anyone. All I knew was I had to get off the stage. And somehow—*somehow*—back to the farm, where I would try to muddle through the lonely days and torturous nights.

Two Years Later

THE DARK CLOUD hovered over north central Tennessee like the hand of an angry God. For two days it had rained, just as it had that night. For two days there had not been any sign of the storms letting up or moving on. On the third day of rain, which was three years to the day since Billy's murder, I decided the rain was a sign.

I was determined to end the anguish. Stop the nightmares. There would be no more dreaming about love and sunshine, only to wake in the morning with the knowledge it would never again be true. No more dreaming about a life cut down by a killer's bullet.

I was full up with pain. So full of bitterness and sorrow, the will to go on had left me. Nothing made sense without Billy. No amount of begging God or making deals with the devil would bring him back. All my efforts at moving forward and getting on with my life had failed. I couldn't eat. Hardly slept. Didn't work. I was living on Billy's life insurance, but I was smart enough, even in my grief, to know it couldn't last forever.

Late that afternoon I pulled on a pair of Billy's sweatpants. They hung on me, even with the drawstring waist pulled tight— only my jutting hipbones kept them from pooling around my ankles. I dug around the laundry basket for a camisole and covered it with Billy's matching hoodie. I slipped my feet into a pair of running shoes, tied the laces, grabbed my hobo purse from the doorknob of our master bedroom, and shuffled outside to Billy's old truck.

I made the drive to Nashville that evening, as I had three years earlier. Nothing was different. I was soaked through and through, just like before. My headlights revealed only rain as it beat down on the asphalt in wide sheets. As before, I was heading for the alleyway behind Murphy's Liquor Store.

By the time I turned onto the street, the rain had let up a bit. The lights from the old Ford cut through the darkness. No one stirred along the sidewalks or under the awnings. The streetlamps flickered, but the lights inside the stores were dim. I parked the truck directly in front of Murphy's.

I unlatched the glove compartment, watching my breath form little clouds that floated toward the dashboard. I reached in and quickly pulled out the .44 Magnum that Billy had kept tucked inside. I took out a box of bullets, dropping it onto the seat beside me. I opened the box and removed one bullet.

Just one.

I only needed one.

After several short, rapid breaths, I opened the door and stepped out of the truck, onto the rain-slicked sidewalk. I didn't bother to close the door. What would be the point? Stench from a nearby Dumpster permeated the air, but it didn't deter me. I kept moving, past the bar-covered windows and the slum stores, to the gaping mouth of the alleyway.

The passageway between the dark buildings looked as dismal as it had three years ago. I stood there looking at the spot where Billy's blood had spilled onto the road, where he'd taken his last breath . . . only a few feet from another Dumpster, as though he'd been worth less than a piece of trash.

Before moving into the alleyway, I wondered—as I had for three years—what his final thoughts had been. Had he thought of me? Or had the killer done his deed so quickly, Billy's life had simply . . . ended. I wondered if there had been much pain. If he'd felt the bullet tear through his heart. Or if, graciously, he'd felt nothing at all.

And I wondered again where God had been in those moments. Where was the great Master of the world when evil had been allowed to triumph and good had been consigned to die?

I staggered a bit to the spot where Billy had died. I dropped to my knees, then my chest, and finally laid my cheek against the cold, wet asphalt. Dirt in the street had turned to mud. I felt it grind into my cheeks, abrasively. But I didn't care.

The smell of gasoline and oil lingered, meshing with the scent of rain in the city. Fat drops of it stung my head and my hands. As much as I'd come to hate the rain—for what it had cost me, for calling Billy out that night and into this godforsaken part of town—I didn't care. I closed my eyes and imagined myself as Billy, blood oozing from my body, life slipping from my lungs.

When I opened my eyes, I found my finger had wrapped around the trigger of the pistol. I pulled myself up to stand. Billy's jacket and sweats weighed heavy on my body as I moved to a cinderblock wall, turned, and leaned against it. I opened the cylinder of the gun and shoved the single bullet into the uppermost chamber. I closed the chamber, and it clicked shut. I slid downward until I was sitting, knees at my chest, feet pressed together. I swallowed twice, raised the pistol, and pushed the cold muzzle against the wet skin under my chin.

I squeezed my eyes shut, drew one last breath, and whispered a final word.

"Billy."

My hand began to shake.

Was I cold? Afraid?

No. *No.* I was doing this. I was ending it. Whatever pain resulted from the bullet entering my brain was nothing compared to what I lived with on a daily basis. I had to . . . had to . . .

Right now. Right—

A thump and a scream from the street beyond the alley caused my eyes to fly open. I turned toward it, dropping the gun to the street beside me.

"*Keisha!*" A boy's cry rose above the pounding of rain. "*Keisha!*"

I grabbed the gun, slipped it into my jacket pocket. I began to run. Faster . . . faster, until I could see the front of Murphy's. The streetlamp shone down on the crumpled body of a little girl who appeared to be no more than six.

Another child, a boy of about nine—dark-blue hoodie pulled over his head, backpack balanced on his back, white teeth bared against wet, dark skin—cried out her name again. "*Keisha!*"

I stopped in front of him, frozen. He saw me then, his eyes wild, his hands laid over the girl as though she were the most prized thing in the world. "She—she got hit," he hollered into the rain. "By that car. She got hit!"

I jogged the distance remaining between us, scooped the child into my arms, felt the warmth of her blood seeping between my fingers, the weight of her head against my shoulder. One hand lay against my chest, quivering. She was beautiful. And unconscious.

"That's my truck," I said to the boy. "Get in."

He scooped up a lavender vinyl backpack I'd not noticed before. "You know where the hospital's at?" he asked, sliding into the passenger's side of the truck.

"Here, you'll have to hold her," I said, laying the girl in his lap. I pulled the seat-belt buckle over the two of them. After I heard it click, I jerked it to make sure it was secure.

"Well? Do ya?" the boy asked me again, his voice filled with fear. "Do you know where the hospital is?"

I didn't. "Do you?"

"Naw, man! Naw."

I looked up the street and then down. There was no one. Nothing was open. I'd left my cell phone at home. "Don't worry," I said. "We'll find it." I shut the door. Precious time was wasting.

THE CORRIDOR OUTSIDE the emergency room's patient area was long and dimly lit. Old plastic chairs, gurneys, wheelchairs, and a short line of oxygen tanks lined the narrow space. I sat with my elbows on my knees, my face in my hands, looking down at my feet, pressed together on the dingy white linoleum. My shoes were still wet. I was still wet. And I was tired. And alive. I had set out to do one thing that evening, and I'd failed.

"Ms. Crawford?"

I looked into the face of young nurse, a wisp of a woman, really. She wore her dark hair pulled back in a chignon. Her honey-colored face was pretty and devoid of makeup with the exception of shadow over her lids, which made her almond-shaped eyes appear all the larger. She rested an elbow on the countertop of the nurses' station, appearing completely relaxed about the trauma I'd rushed into her shift.

"How is she?" My words came like a whisper. I was nearly too exhausted to speak.

"She got banged up pretty good. She's got a mild concussion, and we had to put some stitches in her forehead." She touched her own near the hairline. "We're gonna keep her overnight to be safe, but she should be just fine."

"Did you reach the family?"

"Someone should be here any minute."

I breathed a sigh of relief, not only at the news that Keisha would be okay, but that—if family were coming—I could go home. Home, where I knew I'd be forced to reevaluate things in light of the night's events. I reached for my purse, which I'd thrown onto the chair next to me.

"Ms. Crawford?" the nurse said.

I looked up again.

"The police are downstairs. Waitin' for a statement. But if you got a second, the little girl wants to see you."

I clutched the purse close to my chest. Nodded.

"Room twenty-seven," she said, looking down the hallway. "Down that way, turn right."

I nodded again, stood, and followed the directions until I came to the open door of the girl's room. I peered in. Keisha lay sleeping in the bed, covered by a sheet and a thin blue blanket. She looked so helpless, so fragile. A gauze bandage covered the side of her forehead. Her brother sat in a chair beside the bed, arms hanging limp. His hands were cupped over his knees. The book bag he'd carried earlier sat atop a table beneath the window, beyond which the night had managed to carry on without us.

Seeing me in the doorway, he looked up. "Hey," he said.

"Hey yourself."

"She wanted to tell you something." The boy stood, reached over the raised rails of the bed, touched his sister's shoulder, and shook gently.

"No, no . . . no. Don't wake her. She needs her rest."

He stopped, walked around the bed, saying, "She's goin' be mad if she don't get to see you." When he stood directly before me, he stopped. "So then what about tomorrow?"

"Tomorrow?"

"You comin' tomorrow?"

Coming tomorrow, I thought. Back . . . here?

"I don't know," I said. Then again, what else did I have to do? "I think so. I think I'd like that. Yes."

He narrowed his eyes and tilted his head as though he were studying a work of modern art he couldn't understand. "How do I know you not playin'?"

I couldn't help but notice the tough-boy attitude in the way he spoke out of the side of his mouth, like a little Cagney of his time. "I . . . uh . . ." I reached my hand into the hobo bag, to the front pocket where I kept my business cards. I'd put several of them in before leaving home that evening. For the police, for when they found my body.

I drew one out and handed it to him. "Here."

He studied it for a moment. "Samantha Crawford."

"Sam. You can call me Sam. And what's your name?"

His eyes never left mine. "I'm Macon. And you just made me a promise."

Macon extended his hand to seal the deal.

I slipped mine over his. "Well, I guess I did," I said, not breaking contact, easily readjusting my hand to the "second handshake" position.

Macon chuckled and, somehow, I managed to smile myself.

"All right then," I said.

"All right. See you tomorrow."

I squeezed his hand once more. "Good night, Macon. Tell Keisha I'll be back."

"Tomorrow."

"Tomorrow."

I left the doorway—I'd never really made it into the room— and started back down the corridor, approaching the nurses' station across from where I'd sat minutes before. A black man leaned over it, talking to the same nurse who'd directed me.

My head throbbed. I rubbed my tired eyes with my finger- tips, my feet keeping pace with my heart.

"So she's okay," I heard the man say. His voice was gentle soft. Comforting somehow, despite the fact he was asking for reassurance.

"Yes, sir. She's all right. Gonna be fine. Are you a relative or . . ."

I passed them, intent on getting to the elevators.

"I help look after her," he said. "Ms. Evans is on her way up now."

"What's your name, honey?"

"Joe," he said. "Joe Bradford."

Joe Bradford? I turned. Looked at the man.

Caramel-colored skin. Dark mop of hair. Handsome face.

Could it be . . .

"Joe Bradford?" I asked.

He turned, his face fully directed toward me, leaving little doubt. Those were his eyes, all right. Kind. Gentle. Full of grace. The mischief had been replaced by weariness, but they were his all the same.

"Yes." His expression, or lack thereof, told me he didn't recognize me at all.

"It's me. Sam. Samantha Thomas."

His mouth dropped open, and his brow rose. "Sam?" He chuckled as his arms reached for me, mine doing the same for him. We held each other, both laughing, both amazed by the moment.

"How have you been, girl?"

I studied his face. "I can't believe it's you."

"What are you doing here?" When he saw Keisha's dried blood on my hands, he took them in his and said, "Are you okay?"

The nurse said, "This is the lady who brought the children here."

Joe drew back. "You have got to be kidding me. Of all the people. Where you living at, girl?"

"About twenty miles out of town. And look at you. Samurai Joe, all grown up and living in the big city after all."

"Yeah, something like that," he answered with a half smile.

I realized the implication of his previous words, the ones he'd spoken before I'd interrupted him and the nurse. He was there about Keisha and Macon.

"Are Keisha and Macon your kids?"

He dipped his chin. "Well, now . . . that's complicated."

The nurse leaned in. "I take it you two know each other."

Joe looked from her to me. "This lady right here was my best friend when we were kids." He reached for me again as the station phone rang. "Come here, girl."

I stepped into his arms one more time. It felt good, being there. Being held. Especially by someone I loved and trusted, even if I hadn't seen him in forever.

"Station three," the nurse answered. "Yes, sir . . . she's right here. I'll send her on down."

I knew who it was. The detective, waiting for me downstairs. I prayed it wasn't Detective Miller. It shouldn't be. Should or shouldn't, I couldn't bear to see him again. Not tonight. Not this night.

"You got a real impatient detective down there," the nurse said with a smile.

"I gotta go," I said to Joe.

"Wait, wait." Joe's hand touched my arm. "You got a card or something?"

For the second time that night, I reached into my bag and pulled out a card. This time, the opening was wide enough that I could see the barrel of the gun resting at the bottom.

"It's a little wet," I said, removing the card. "Crumpled."

Joe took it, reached over the counter and picked up a pink sticky pad. The nurse handed him her pen. I watched as he scribbled his name and address onto it, tore off the top sheet, and handed it to me. "You come see me if you can. We got a lot of catching up to do."

Another invitation for me to return. Two in one night. Something inside me stirred. Something that felt a little like renewed purpose, but it was too early to be sure. "It was good to see you, Joe."

"You too."

I turned and walked away from my old friend, my eyes reading the address Joe had given me.

"You come see me, now," he repeated.

I turned to look over my shoulder. Studying him, I could tell he really wanted me to do just that. Yes, purpose—a reason to keep going—might be what I was feeling after all. "I will," I said.

And I meant it.

Chapter Four

ON THE WAY home I thought about the day Joe and I met back at Hazelwood Elementary School. It was on a Wednesday, during lunch period. I don't know how or why I remember the day, but I do.

The third-, fourth-, and fifth-grade classes had just settled into place along the rows of bench tables.

I was different from most of the kids I went to school with. More of a dreamer. So I usually sat at the far end of the room, near the wall, keeping to myself as much as possible. Unfortunately, that day like so many others, Jimmy Legg had managed to sit across from me.

Jimmy was a bully. He had a head full of blond hair, which he wore combed back as though he were some kind of hoodlum from the 1950s. A Fonzie throwback from *Happy Days*. Of course, I didn't realize that then. I only came to understand it later.

We'd been sitting long enough for Jimmy to taunt me, to pick on me because I was snaggle-toothed and scrawny. Back then I thought he was the meanest boy in the world. Today I realize he may have been a little bit infatuated with me and had acted as boys will when they "like" a girl.

"Go away, Jimmy," I said. "I don't want you to eat lunch with me."

But before he could retort, our principal, Mrs. Gray, called for everyone to be quiet. I looked past the rows of students—each of the girls trying to look more like Madonna than the others, and the boys imitating Michael Jackson's style—to where she stood in front of the food line. Standing next to her, looking sad and scared, was a caramel-skinned boy with a darker mop of hair, bushy around his head with little ringlets sticking out here and there. He neither smiled nor frowned, and I couldn't help but wonder who he was and what he was doing at our mostly white school.

"Everyone," Mrs. Gray called out, clapping her hands, waiting for the murmuring to die down completely. She placed her fingertips where a secondhand book bag hung from the boy's shoulder, as if she dared to only half touch him.

I raised myself slightly so I could see all of him. He wore a gold tee over a long-john shirt and charcoal-colored pants. In one hand he carried a rumpled brown paper bag, in the other a piece of paper. Probably his class schedule, I figured. From clear over where I was sitting, I could see it quivering next to his hip.

He sure looked funny standing there. No doubt he felt funny, too, as the only black child in a room full of whites. "Everyone," Mrs. Gray said again, "this is Joe Bradford. His grandmother is the new custodian." She swallowed hard, and her face pinched. She gave us that look that said she was about to make a new rule, one we'd better follow. "I want you *all* to make him feel welcome."

No one said a word. They just stared at him and him back at them.

Mrs. Gray pushed him forward. "Run along and find a seat," she said.

I didn't yet know a lot about race relations, or lack thereof, but even at eight years of age, I knew that wasn't going to be an easy task. The other kids started putting their lunch boxes and books wherever a space might have been for Joe to sit. He finally made his way to the back of the room, to the seat next to where Jimmy sat across from me. Jimmy turned, put his hand down between where he and his best friend, Bart Atkins, sat.

"Seat's taken," he said.

I kept on looking at the new boy, this Joe Bradford, wondering what it must feel like to be new in a school, to be a different color from everyone else. I also wondered what kind of food he had in his lunch bag. My mama had packed Jell-O in mine, even though I'd told her a thousand times how much I didn't like it. No matter how many times I'd told her that what I really wanted with my turkey-and-cheese sandwich was potato chips, she always packed Jell-O.

I guess Joe had nowhere else to go. In spite of Jimmy's warning, Joe walked over and sat down there anyway. Next thing I knew, all the boys sitting on that side of the table had gotten up and left, which was fine with me.

Joe hung his head, resting it in his free hand, looking about as rejected and alone as anyone I'd ever seen.

I looked at the brown bag on the table, still gripped tightly in his other hand. The grand possibility of potato chips somewhere within the recesses of that bag kept me from being shy or silent.

"Whatcha got?" I asked.

He cocked one eye toward me.

"Got something to trade?" I continued.

"Oh." He opened the bag, dumped out a sandwich bag filled with a fat peanut-butter-and-jelly sandwich, another bag with what appeared to be a soggy dill pickle, and a bag of Golden Flake potato chips.

I felt hope rise inside. "You like Jell-O?"

"Yeah."

"Well then, how about my Jell-O for your tater chips?"

Joe's dark eyes considered my orange Jell-O cup, then roamed back to his bag of chips and again to my side of the table. "Okay."

"By the way, my name's Samantha, but you can call me Sam."

"Hey, Sam. I'm Joe."

"I know." When his brow furrowed, I added, "Mrs. Gray said so when you were up there at the front of the room with her."

"Oh, yeah."

We ate without another word.

At the end of lunch period, he smiled at me. "Maybe we can trade again tomorrow," he said, standing and gathering his belongings.

I did the same, tossing empty sandwich and potato chip bags into my pink kitty cat lunchbox. "Okay," I said. "It's a deal." I reached my hand across the table. It was a daring thing to do. What little bit I knew about blacks and whites fell right into that category.

And I'm sure Joe knew it too. But he slipped his hand in mine, bringing them down one time before turning his hand so his fingers clasped mine around the back.

I learned a whole new way of shaking on a deal that day, and I never forgot it, even when making a deal with Macon.

A FULL MOON hung low over the barn, lighting the path as I pulled the old Ford truck beside it. I was still deep in thought, thinking about how—later that first day of our friendship, at the start of recess—Joe had been sitting outside on the playground, reading a Samurai comic book. When I saw him sitting on the bench reading, I called to him from the top of the steps. "Hey, Joe!"

He looked up and smiled. Waved back at me as I did the same. It felt good knowing I'd made a new friend, especially one who liked comic book stories. I already wanted to share with him some of my own drawings and stories. As I bounded down the stairs, Jimmy and Bart and some other boys came around the corner. Jimmy stuck his foot out, catching my ankle and hurling me forward. I hit the gravel, my arms thrown out in front of me, my long red hair flying. The rocks dug into my knees and palms. Bad as I didn't want to, I started to cry.

Joe was in front of Jimmy before I had a chance to get up. "Who tripped her?" he demanded.

"She's your girlfriend," Jimmy shot back. "Why don't you make her tell you!"

I'd managed to stand by then and was making every effort to get out of the way. The boys had fisted their hands, and they circled each other, ready for a fight. My earlier hope now turned to fear, fear for my new friend. For what these boys—who easily outnumbered him—could and would do to him.

"Joe, no!" I said, but I don't think he heard me.

"I'm only gonna tell you this once," Jimmy said. "And I'm gonna talk *real slow* so you can understand me. It'll be a cold day in Jamaica before some ni—"

Joe's fist cracked into Jimmy's nose so fast, no one saw it coming. Jimmy went down in an instant and, when he did, Joe was on top of him, pounding his fist into Jimmy's face. Everyone but me started yelling, "Fight! Fight! Fight!" until some of the grownups came running over and separated the two boys.

The three of us—Jimmy, Joe, and me—got called into Mrs. Gray's office. She had me come in first. I remember how frightened I was, sitting across from that big desk, legs swinging from the seat of a chair three times too big for me. My knees were covered in bloody scrapes, the pads of my hands throbbing. She asked me to tell her the truth about what happened, and I did. I told her how Jimmy had tripped me and how Joe, my new friend, had come to my rescue. "I don't think Jimmy likes Joe, Mrs. Gray," I said. "But you should know that Joe's a real nice boy."

Mrs. Gray smiled at me. "I'm sure he is, honey. What I want you to do now is walk on down to the nurse's office. She'll put something on those boo-boos for you."

"Yes, ma'am."

I hobbled out of the room and into the wide hallway bathed in semidarkness and lined with lockers. Joe and Jimmy sat on a single bench with about four feet between them. I stopped long enough to look at Joe but not at Jimmy. "See you at lunch tomorrow?" I asked.

Joe gave me a crooked smile. "Yeah."

I smiled back. "Don't forget my tater chips."

"I won't," he said.

And he didn't.

I PULLED THE gun from the hobo bag and held it loosely in my hand as though I hadn't really expected to find it there. Light shining from the moon and the lamp over the barn door came together, illuminating the dark of the pistol's grip.

What was I going to do now? Try again? Here? In this truck? Billy's truck? It wouldn't be the same. Go back to the alley behind Murphy's? I'd have to wait another year for that to make sense, which was about as illogical a thought as any of the others I'd been having lately.

Keisha's blood had dried between my fingers and around my cuticles, and I could see it on the hand that was wrapped around the gun. How was it, I wondered, that those children had been out so late at night? And what were the odds of Keisha getting hit in front of my truck?

Billy's truck. Always, always . . . Billy's truck.

What's more, what were the odds of her being somehow related to Joe?

What was it he'd said when I asked him about it? *That's complicated.*

A stepfather, maybe? Or an uncle? Joe didn't have any siblings that I knew of, but Keisha and Macon could be the niece and nephew of his wife. If he was married. He hadn't said, and I hadn't asked.

I placed the gun back in the glove compartment, slammed the door shut, got out of the truck, and called for Billy's horse, who I could see stood nearby, by making kissing noises. She ambled up from the north side of the barn, her mocha-colored mane and tail shimmering in the moonlight. Just being near her made me feel that much closer to Billy.

She nuzzled my shoulder. "Hey, Cricket," I said. I stroked her forehead and leaned over to kiss the top of her muzzle. "How's my girl?"

I ran my hand up her cheek, down to her shoulder. I stepped closer, laid my head against her, drew in the scent of horse and hay. Billy. "Strange day today, huh?" I asked, as though she had been with me from start to finish.

My purse hung heavy in my hand as I walked into the barn, past a few bales of hay and some small farm equipment, and through the area where Billy had done his woodworking. His "thinking hobby," he called it. I'd not touched a single item since he'd died. The wood shavings, the hand tools, the half-finished birdhouse—it was all there.

Over on the wall, mounted, was the first big fish Billy had reeled in when he was a boy. Too big for eating, his daddy had said. This was the kind you show off. We'd had a playful tug of war over it after we married, Billy teasing me that we should hang it over our bed, while I was determined it would reside absolutely nowhere in our house.

Oh, God . . . if you'd just let him come back for one hour, I'd hang it anywhere he wanted. I swear. Just one hour.

I stepped over to where Billy had kept the record player that had been with him since high school, and an 8-track tape player he kept "just in case they ever come back." We'd bought a locker at Home Depot, a place for Billy to keep his box of LPs by Hank Sr., Loretta Lynn, and Kitty Wells—a honky-tonk heaven on vinyl if ever there was one. After he died, I hung Billy's work jacket and his army duffel bag over the open door of the locker and set his scuffed white hard hat on the table beside them.

On a whim, I removed the jacket, pressed it to my face, and inhaled. It was losing his scent, though I could still make it out if I tried. A single tear slipped down my cheek, whether because of my losing Billy or the jacket losing his scent, I don't know. Maybe a little of both. I hung it up again and then allowed my fingers to skip over the scratches along the top of the helmet. I walked to the bottom of the stairs, flipped a switch, and waited the millisecond it took before the loft's lights flickered on.

With a sigh, I started the climb, one step at a time, feeling as though my body weight was more than I could carry. Stopping at the top, I allowed myself to take the room in. I hadn't been here in nearly a year. Cobwebs billowed from the corners of the ceiling. Framed covers of my books and awards hung on open studs. Along one wall, my paints and pencils stood in white containers, faithfully waiting for their artist to return. Empty Mason jars for washing out my brushes collected dust in a corner. Nearby was the drawing I'd pretended to be so interested in the day Billy had come home to chickens in the coffee mug cabinet, kept warm by a thick blanket of dust and neglect. The old farm kitchen table that doubled as my work station stood scarred and forgotten. Overhead was the chalkboard where Billy had always left love notes for me.

DANCE LIKE NO ONE'S WATCHING.

WHO LOVES YOU MORE THAN ME?

PLEASE, PLEASE GO TO THE BANK TODAY.

DON'T FORGET MY JEFFERSONS IF U R GOING 2 TOWN.

The last one he'd written had not been erased. Would *never* be erased.

THIS WILL BE YOUR BEST ONE YET. LOVE ALWAYS, B.

Pinned to the large corkboard under the chalkboard was a photograph of Billy and me. Him sitting on a hay bale, me behind him, arms draped over his shoulders. If I closed my eyes, I could still feel the warmth of his skin, the soft cotton of his shirt.

I drew in a shaky breath and let it go as I moved closer to the corkboard. Sketches I'd been working on were now covered by the ones I'd drawn the year after Billy died.

A dark man in a red hoodie. Back turned, faceless head twisted. Looking back. Taunting me. Daring me to know who he was. Why he had killed Billy.

A dark alley, lined with Dumpsters against block walls. Billy's blood pooled in the center. Yellow tape cordoning off the spot where a lifeless body lay.

The front of Murphy's Liquor Store, where Billy had made his last work call.

The place where I had hoped, just hours ago, to die too.

Chapter Five

BRIGHT SUNSHINE SPILLED through the gauzy lace curtains that draped over floor-to-ceiling bedroom windows. Morning songbirds had been chirping for hours, but for the most part I'd ignored them, pulling the thick quilts up high and burrowing beneath them. The night before I'd placed my cell phone on top of a book my mother insisted would help me in my time of grief. Mostly the book was gathering dust on the small bedside table.

When the phone rang, I pushed back the covers, raked strands of hair from across my eyes, and reached into the chill of the room for the phone. I nearly knocked over the horse-shaped lamp, grabbed at it to keep it steady, and looked at the caller ID.

Unknown Caller.

I'd left my number with the hospital. Thinking it could be a nurse updating me about Keisha, I answered. "Hello?"

Sirens blared in the background. City life met my ears before I heard an angry boy say, "You broke your promise."

This was definitely not Keisha's nurse. "What?"

"And you owe me a quarter for this call I'm making."

I rolled onto my back, now recognizing the caller. "Macon. No. No, I'm still coming up there."

"Too late. They done sent us home."

I pushed the covers off me, swung my legs over the bed, and dropped my feet onto the wide pine floorboards where my dusty footprints made a path from the door to the bed, from the bed to the closet. "You're home?"

"Yeah. And you just made a big. Fat. Liar outta me."

"Uh . . ." I darted across the room to my dresser, jerked open the top drawer, and pulled out a ribbed long-sleeved tee.

"'Cause I told Keisha you was comin' to see her."

His voice was raised. Angry. I looked at the '70s throwback wall clock. It was nearly eleven. He had every right to be mad.

"Looked her in the eye!" he continued.

I thought I heard him giggle, but it could have been a sob. "Macon, I am so, so sorry . . ." I grabbed the pair of jeans I'd hooked over the end of the wrought iron bed—mine and Billy's with its heart-shaped railings across the footboard and head-board—stepped into them and said, "Actually I was just on my way to the hospital. I wanted to stop by and pick up something special for Keisha."

"Something special?"

I put the phone on speaker, tossed it on the bed, and kept talking. "Absolutely."

An old brass coat rack—one Billy and I found at a flea market and bought for under five dollars—stood next to the window. One of my cotton shirts hung next to the one Billy had worn the day before he'd been killed. I reached for it. "What would she like?"

"Well, whatcha got? Maybe some candy?"

I dug my arms into the sleeves, and adjusted the shirt on my shoulders. "Sure. What kind does she like?"

"Bring her some Reese's. And some M&Ms. I *love*—I mean, she *love* them things."

"I can do that." I stood in front of the gilded mirror that had come out of Billy's grandmother's house and started brushing my hair before catching it into a low ponytail and tying it off with a scrunchie.

"And *pizza!*" he said, almost too excitedly. "Bring some pizza." He paused. "With ham and mushrooms."

"I just need your address," I said, digging in my purse for something to write with.

He gave it to me. "It's in the Commons. The projects," he said. "You know where *that* is?"

I didn't know *exactly*, but I figured it had to be close to Murphy's and that my GPS would take me there. "It'll take me about forty-five minutes to get there, okay?" I said, totally guessing.

"Just don't forget to come."

"I won't. I promise."

OTHER THAN LAST night and the night Billy died, I'd never been on that side of town. And never in the daytime. East Nashville. Poverty rose around me like the stink from the over-flowing Dumpsters. White-framed houses looking as though they would collapse under their own weight ran along both sides of the streets. Busted windows were replaced by cardboard or sheets of particleboard. Fat, paint-sprayed graffiti tainted some of the homes, bringing the only hint of color to an otherwise gray existence. Chain-linked fences—some without the chain-link—separated the sand-spewed sidewalks from the dirt-filled yards where, if any grass dared to grow, it was soon choked out.

I drove past a recreational area that was nothing more than a concrete slab enclosed by a two-foot-tall brick fence. About six boys played basketball around a hoop with no net, while at least twice that many scantily dressed girls sat on the bricks, legs crossed, watching their every move. My window was down, and I could hear hip-hop music playing from somewhere, nearly drowning the calls of the girls.

"All right, now!"

"Get it in there, Tyree! Shut it down!"

I rolled my car to a stop at the sign, looked beyond the girls and the players long enough to see a group of three boys standing in front of an abandoned house where the front porch had caved in. They seemed to sense me staring at them, and they turned and glared my way.

My breath caught in my throat. Not at the obvious loitering around a crack house, but that all three wore red hoodies.

The car behind me honked, startling me.

My GPS had told me to turn left and I did, taking me right past the boys. They continued glaring at me, their expressions making it clear that I didn't belong there. Nervous, I looked straight ahead and noticed a crooked, green street sign: WHITE STREET.

"Turn right," the navigator told me.

I swallowed hard as I continued my way up the street, looking for 1820. I found it on the left but kept going; the smell of pizza from the passenger's seat told me I had something else to do first.

Besides, there wasn't any way this house on White Street could be Joe's.

It just couldn't be.

THE ADDRESS MACON had given me was a grouping of neglected two-story, Colonial-style brick buildings that appeared to hold six apartments each. The structures ran around the perimeter of the block, their backs creating a common area in the center where clothes billowed on wires stretched this way and that. The scents of detergent and fabric softener blended with the pungency of both stale and fresh cigarette smoke and Dumpster trash. Somewhere, someone was smoking a joint—the odor of it wafted through the air where children played on primary-colored playground equipment. Near them, young black mothers stared at the red-haired white woman carrying a pizza box and a bag full of candy.

Along the stoops outside the barred doors and windows, older women sat in cast-off kitchen and living room chairs. One such woman—thin and frail with brows arched over suspicious eyes— looked emptily in my direction. She pulled a cigarette out of a pack sitting next to a bottle of liquor wrapped in a brown paper bag. Wind chimes above her head tinkled in the breeze. The woman looked up as she struck a match that instantly went out. As I neared her, I heard her lament over what was obviously her last one.

"Well, how 'bout that," she said when I got near enough to hear. "She *did* come."

The storm door of the apartment burst open with Macon running through it. Keisha hobbled behind him. I smiled at her, and she weakly returned the gesture. She looked much better than she had the night before. Her hair had been brushed into two large pigtails that danced whimsically on both sides of her face. She wore a pair of jean shorts, a pink tee, and a lightweight jacket. Macon sported jeans and a bright-green polo shirt. They were both clearly happy to see me.

"'Bout time you showed up!" Macon said, grabbing the pizza and candy from my hands.

"Well, it's nice to see you too," I said, somewhat taken aback by his brazenness.

"Boy, you better mind your manners!" the woman warned.

"We were 'bout to fall over, man," he said, dropping the box and the sack to the cement stoop before sitting beside it, tearing into the candy first.

Keisha remained in front of me. I saw a small pad of paper in one hand, a black colored pencil in the other.

"Hi, Keisha. Remember me?" I asked, squatting down to better see her. My eyes swept over the bandage along her forehead. I wanted to touch it but didn't dare.

She nodded, eyes never leaving mine until she started writing something on the pad. When she turned it toward me, I read: YOU HELPED US.

I couldn't help but wonder why she wrote rather than spoke, but I nodded without questioning it. "Yes, I did." I smiled. "It's nice to meet you, Keisha. I'm Sam."

Keisha gave me a sweet smile, stronger than the one before.

"Keisha," the woman called. "You better get on over here if you want any-a this."

Keisha turned to see that her brother had already fairly well devoured much of the candy I'd brought. He'd also opened the pizza box and had removed a slice.

"Boy," the woman continued. "You act like you ain't never seen pizza nor candy before."

Macon's mouth was so full, he could only roll his eyes. Keisha shook her tiny head and moseyed over to join him. I stood, daring to look at the woman who did nothing to hide her attempt at sizing me up.

She laid the butt of the unlit cigarette between her lips. "Name's Mattie," she said around it. "It's a good thing whatcha done fo' my babies."

"Anybody would have done it."

She guffawed, pulling the cigarette from between her lips. "No. Dey wouldn't."

Mattie turned to look down the sidewalk where I continued to stand. I followed her gaze. A thickly-muscled man was stepping onto the stoop of an apartment in the building next door, heading inside. "Hey, T! You got a light?"

"T" wore a pair of dark-blue Dickies stained with motor oil. His shirt—a lighter shade of blue but just as blemished—bore a patch with name "Anthony" on the right and another with "Nashville Motorcars" on the left. He ambled toward us as though he had all the time in the world, and his eyes focused on me. He wore a do-rag on his head, a scowl on his face, and he rolled a Black & Mild cigar between his lips. He reached behind him, pulled a red mechanic's rag from a back pocket, and wiped his hands with it before digging into his shirt pocket for a lighter.

A red mechanic's rag. Just like the one dropped next to Billy's body by his murderer. My heart thudded in my chest.

I blinked at the sound of a dog barking nearby, bringing me back to where Anthony's Zippo flickered under Mattie's cigarette. The traffic from the streets sounded like waves rushing to a shoreline.

"You are a prince among thieves, T," Mattie said. "A prince among thieves."

He cast me a sideward glance before turning to go back to his apartment, swaggering as he went.

"Can I go hang with T a while?" Macon asked.

Mattie looked concerned. "Boy, leave that man alone."

But Macon was undaunted. "Can I, T?" he hollered.

T opened the storm door to his place, looked inside then back to us. "Whatever."

Macon gathered candy wrappings and what was left of my gift for Keisha before scrambling to the other building and disappearing inside.

"Sometimes I wanna slap that boy's hair white," Mattie muttered.

I smiled, but when I turned to see Keisha looking into a lone bag of Reese's and finding it empty, I sighed. Mattie shook her head. "That boy . . ."

I reached into my purse and brought out the pink sticky note Joe had given me the night before. I cast a glance over my shoulder in the direction of where I'd parked. "How far does this road go?"

"Four more streets, and then it dead end."

I looked at Mattie. She drew on her cigarette, blew the smoke upward, eyes squinting. "Help you find something?"

I handed her the note. "I passed this address on the way here. It's supposed to be my friend's house, but . . . but I'm not sure."

"Let me see," Mattie said, extending her hand. "Mm-hmm." She looked at me cautiously. "Gray siding? Peeling paint?"

I nodded. "Yeah."

"You friends with Joe Bradford?"

I squared my shoulders. "Why, yes, ma'am."

Mattie chuckled. "Well, you in luck. 'Cause that's where he lives."

She handed the paper back to me. I took it, a million new questions running through my mind, but only one that mattered: *How had Joe ended up here?*

Mattie read my thoughts. "Welcome to the projects, honey," she said with another chuckle. "Welcome to the projects."

Chapter Six

BACK IN MY car, I retraced my earlier course until, two streets over, I reached Joe's house. I pulled my car to a stop directly in front and instinctively locked the door as I stepped out. The house was, by far, the nicest one on the block, despite the peeling paint, one cracked window, and another with a board running diagonally on the inside—a poor man's home invasion deterrent.

A chain-link fence ran along the front of the yard. It was bent in places, rusty in others. A beat-up mailbox with the words "Papa Joe" painted haphazardly in blue paint stood forlorn at the gate. The red flag drooped permanently earthward.

Yet the yard was warmly inviting. Two folding lawn chairs stood beneath a shade tree. Lush bushes lined the front of the house, and colorful potted plants decorated each step up to the front porch and then along the railing. I saw that the front door was wide open, but the storm door was shut. I climbed the steps, tilting my head, listening to the sound of jazz coming from inside. The front room was dark, and for the most part I was unable to see much else because child-sized fingerprints marred the glass.

"You're looking for Joe, aren't you?"

I turned, grasping the strap of my purse hanging from my shoulder to keep it from slipping off. A vivacious black woman who appeared to be in her mid-to-late twenties walked toward me from the sidewalk. Her smile was engaging. She was both fashionable and attractive. Before I could answer, she extended her hand, which I took. But instead of shaking my hand, she pulled me into an embrace, hugging me briefly. "He said you might be stopping by," she added, stepping away. "I'm Denise Lyles. I work with Joe."

"Hi. I'm Sam."

Her smile grew larger, if that were at all possible. "I know who you are. He told me all about you." She reached around me, opened the storm door, and said, "Come on in."

I followed Denise into the house.

"Just make yourself at home, and I'll see if I can find Joe," she said, stepping around a corner to the back of the house, leaving me standing just inside the threshold. A moment later the music ceased, leaving me alone in silence.

The living room was sparsely furnished and the wallpaper faded, but everything was clean. Tidy. I listened for Joe's voice— or Denise's—but heard nothing. I stepped shyly toward the corner Denise had disappeared around. I saw it led down a long hallway. Unsure, but too curious to stay put, I decided to see where it led, but not before stopping at a faux-wood bookshelf against the living room wall. The shelves were stacked with multicolored construction paper, Mason jars, Solo cups, and Elmer's Glue bottles. Some of the jars held gum balls. Others crayons or paints. Inside the cups were colored pencils, Popsicle sticks, and paint brushes.

The walls of the hallway were made up of scuffed paneling on the bottom and green-painted sheetrock on the top, separated by thin chair-railing. The upper half of one wall was filled with children's drawings, mounted with thumb tacks. Each one was signed to "Papa Joe." Among them was one of a little girl holding hands with a man, both standing in a field of blue-green grass under a bright orange-and-yellow sun and happy violet clouds. The name "Keisha" was written next to the girl, "Papa Joe" by the man.

Beside the drawing was a framed photo of Joe and Macon, capturing both in a happy moment, hung crooked. There were a few other framed snapshots, mostly of Joe surrounded by children. I spotted another of him and his grandmother, taken sometime around middle school.

I continued forward, passing a room to the left with a small TV, an oversized chair, and a saxophone resting in its stand nearby. I didn't linger at the door; I was too intrigued by the drawings and finger-paintings on the wall beyond. None were framed but one. I stepped closer to it and smiled.

It was a silly drawing of a boy with an untamed afro, wearing a makeshift martial arts uniform, sword drawn high. Written in the space above him were the words "Samori Joe." I smiled at the memory, of how I'd not known then how to spell "samurai," or, really, how to draw very well.

I took a few more steps, peering into yet another room brightly lit by the afternoon sun streaming through a large window. Inside was a simple double bed, neatly made. Beyond it was a chair with some sort of medical device standing sentry over it. What kind of machine, I couldn't tell. I'd never seen anything like it.

"I knew you'd come."

It was Joe's voice. He stood at the end of the hall, in front of the shelf with the paints and crayons. His hands were loosely tucked into the pockets of his jeans. He wore a light-blue T-shirt under a cotton shirt, and I was about as happy to see him as I'd been to see anyone in a long time. There were so many things I wanted to ask him. To know about him. About the past twenty years.

And about the boys I'd seen wearing red hoodies.

He winked at me, and for a moment I thought he was just as happy to see me as I was him. "I need your help with something."

"Okay."

He walked to where I stood. "It's this way here," he said, pointing past me. "To the kitchen."

I followed him like a lost kitten who'd found a possible new owner.

"Know how to make snow cones?"

"Um . . . no," I said with a light chuckle. "I'm not sure I do."

"That's okay. Denise is here if we need her."

We joined Denise in the kitchen. She stood at the table over two large box tops with tiny slits cut into them and then turned upside down. She shoved Dixie cups filled with crushed ice into each slot. "There you are," she said, smiling at Joe. "Better get a move on."

"I'm there." He walked over to an outdated refrigerator, opened it, and brought out a pitcher filled with red liquid. "Cherry," he said. "They're gonna like this."

Denise smiled at him again. "It wouldn't matter what flavor. It's the point that counts."

I had no idea what they were talking about. I stood in the

doorway between the kitchen and the hall like a rag doll, unsure what to do.

Perhaps sensing my discomfort, Joe handed the pitcher to me. "Here," he said. "Pour a little of this over the ice."

I readjusted the strap of my purse over my shoulder before taking the pitcher and following his instructions. Denise busied herself at the sink while Joe stood over me, watching, saying, "That's good . . . that's good . . ." with the filling of each cup. Once I was done, he took the cherry-flavored liquid, returned it to the refrigerator, and said, "Come on with me."

He picked up one of the box tops. I picked up the other.

Joe glanced casually at his watch. "We're right on time."

I followed behind him back through the house. He opened the front door for me, and I stepped back into the warm sunshine. We walked together down the porch steps to the narrow cement walkway leading to the sidewalk.

Joe took a deep breath beside me. "I bet I know what you're thinking. 'How in the world did Joe end up here?'"

I turned to look at him, following his gaze down the street to where a barely visible school bus was approaching. A line of thin black arms waving rectangles of green paper jutted out from the open windows.

"No." *Yes.* "It's just good to see you, Joe."

"We go this way," Joe said, turning right out of the nonexistent gate in his fence. We took only a few steps before the school bus screeched to a stop in front of us.

The driver, a teddy bear of a man with curly hair peeking out from under a straw cowboy hat and a wide grin below, said, "Hey, Joey!"

"That's Hambrick," Joe said to me. "But we just call him Brick." Joe placed his box on top of mine. "Hold this for me," he said before calling back to the driver. "Brick, my main man!"

Brick stuck a thick, tanned fist out the opened window, which Joe met with his own. "I hope you brought enough, man," Brick said with a laugh. "Your green slips today may outnumber the cups in those trays." The driver glanced my way and smiled at me knowingly. He and I for sure were the only two white people on the block.

Maybe he wondered what in the world I was doing there.

Quite frankly, I wondered the same thing.

Joe laughed easily as the bus door swung open. He bent at the waist, clapping his hands together as though this herd of children racing toward him—backpacks bouncing on their backs, green sheets of paper waving from their hands, white smiles gleaming against the dark of their skin—was the greatest sight on earth.

Who were these kids? More importantly, who was Joe to them?

"What day is it? What day is it?" Joe asked as though gearing up for a cheer.

"Freeze Cup Friday!" they screamed, as they exchanged high fives with Joe.

"Huddle up, huddle up," Joe said as they gathered around him. From their sizes, I estimated their ages to range from about six to twelve. "That's what I'm talkin' about," Joe said to them. "Come on now."

They bunched together like a football team on a playing field. Along with Joe, the children made growling noises, like playful lions getting ready to pounce. The merry-making ended in another wave of cheering. Finally, Joe stood upright and glanced over his shoulder at me. "Green means they had good behavior *all week*." He looked again at the adorable mob with pride. "And for *that?*"

Together they chanted, "It's Freeze Cup Friday!"

Such excitement startled me. I was a children's book writer, but I hadn't been around this many children in more than three years, having chosen to box up and send my books to elementary schools in the projects without participating in their distribution. I raked my teeth over my bottom lip and looked nervously to the bus driver, who chuckled easily at what I'd just witnessed.

"See y'all around," he said. The bus pulled away from the curb with a cough and a sigh.

"Bye, Brick," Joe called. Then to the kids, "Say g'bye."

They waved their green cards, hollering gleefully as the bus rolled away.

Suddenly they all realized at once that a stranger stood among them, holding makeshift trays of freeze cups. A white, nervous stranger.

Joe must have realized it too. He extended his arm, smiling. "Oh, this is my *good friend* from when we were kids, Miss Sam." Eight faces turned fully toward me, eyes wide and unblinking. "Give it up!" Joe cheered.

"Hey, Miss Sam!" they chanted.

Joe burst out laughing.

"Hello," I stammered.

When had I ever seen such joy in the midst of such dire circumstances? And where did it come from? From Joe? Or from just being around him?

That I could imagine. He'd given me years of friendship and contentment when we were children. More than just being funny and kind, Joe had been one of the smartest boys in our school. He'd graduated with honors.

So what was he doing *here?*

THE KIDS GATHERED with Joe and Denise in the backyard. Book bags were tossed onto the half-dozen wooden picnic tables alongside old coffee cans filled with colorful sprays of pansies. At the back of the house, Joe had planted flower beds and bordered them with stone-lined walkways. An ivy-draped chain-link fence ran along both sides of the yard, with a dilapidated wooden privacy fence stretched along the back. All in all, and in spite of being located in the Commons, the yard was manicured, vivid, and at the same time, meant for children.

The snow cones were taken from the box tops and had been inhaled before we ever left the sidewalk. I placed the nearly empty containers on one of the tables, then stood on the sidelines, watching Denise move freely among these angels, talking with them about their week and gathering the green slips of paper and holding them tenderly between her slender fingers.

At some point, Joe dashed toward the back door as though he'd forgotten something inside. As he got close to the steps, he stumbled, but not as though his foot had tripped on a stone or a crack in the cement. This was more like his body had given out, but only for a second. Looking from him to Denise, I saw that the moment had not gone unnoticed by her either. I couldn't help but wonder again about the medical apparatus I'd seen in his room. Something was wrong. I could sense it.

But a minute later he returned, looking vibrant and carrying the saxophone. "Y'all ready?" he called out.

Cheers erupted from the children. They formed a semicircle on either side of Joe and Denise. I remained safely tucked away near a tree so scrawny it would snap in two if I leaned against it for the support I felt I needed. So I held tightly to the strap of my purse instead.

Joe and Denise began a stomp-clap rhythm. The kids joined in and a chant started. "His name is Snuffy, yeah, and he's a clown, yeah, when he gets jiggy, yeah, he break it down! Go, Snuffy! Go, Snuffy . . ."

One of the children, who appeared to be about ten, maybe even as old as twelve, stepped to the center of the half circle. He performed a serious "robot" while the others encouraged him with their clapping and cheering.

I watched, motionless, part of me desperately wanting to be a part of the revelry. Another part refusing. But inside, *something* began to rip. To tear away. Something that had long ago gone numb. Something bitter and confused. I wasn't ready to let it go completely, but the new sensation felt good all the same.

Snuffy returned to the line as the song continued. "His name is Papa, yeah, and he's a clown . . ."

Joe looked at me, eyebrows shooting up in delight. He grinned like a boy in a candy store as the children continued. "Go, Papa! Go, Papa!"

Joe eased into the center of the group, placed his lips around the mouthpiece of the saxophone, and blew a lazy jazz tune. He was immersed wholly in the moment, and I couldn't help but laugh. When he stopped, he faltered again. Around his abdomen, sweat marked his tee in small patches.

Denise leaned over and spoke to him as the children now called on the name of Bernie, keeping rhythm, not missing a beat. Denise's face showed concern. While I could not hear what she said, I could tell it was serious.

Joe shook his head no. Then he nodded and flinched. A nagging feeling washed over me. Something was horribly wrong here. The joy surrounding the children, emanating from their song and laughter, was tainted by something floating just out of reach but coming closer. Something they didn't seem to be aware of.

"Her name is Sam, yeah, and she's a clown . . ."

Attention had suddenly turned to me. I jerked to the reality I may now have to do more than stand on the outside looking in. In their way, the kids were welcoming me into their group, making me one of their own. Trusting me with these moments of their lives. And this scrawny tree couldn't hide me.

Joe threw his hand over his mouth, clearly pleased with this turn of events.

"Go, Sam! Go, Sam! Go, Sam!"

With the exception of the whirring inside my ears, everything grew quiet around me. I couldn't breathe, couldn't find enough air to sustain my lungs' need to expand.

What did these children want from me?

What would I be *required* to give?

"Uh . . ." I said.

The backyard was now completely still. Awkward. The children appeared confused. Joe looked concerned.

Denise was the first to move. "Uh . . . uh-uh! Uh . . . uh-uh!" She swayed from side to side, creating a new song and the dance that went with it.

She smiled as the children joined her. "Uh . . . uh-uh! Uh . . . uh-uh!" they shouted until everyone doubled over with laughter.

Joe extended his arms outward, smiling sympathetically. "And the white girl goes down in flames," he teased, clapping.

The kids applauded, and I breathed a sigh of relief. I nodded my thanks toward Denise, who winked in return. I looked to Joe for a sign of what I was supposed to do next, but he didn't seem to read my thoughts.

"All right," Denise said. "Homework!"

"Awww . . ."

"Let's go. C'mon! Get your book bags."

The children found their places without further argument. Denise and Joe had obviously been working with them for some time. Books, paper, and pencils were pulled from the book bags and deposited unceremoniously onto the tables. Denise began to walk around them, quietly orchestrating "homework time."

I found a place at an unoccupied table and sat to observe. Joe joined me there.

"So, what have you been up to, girl?"

"Nothing really."

"C'mon now. You can't say that. I saw it on your business card. You're a children's book author?"

I shook my head. "No. I mean, yes. I was. But I . . . I stopped writing three years ago."

Joe's brow furrowed, the pain in his eyes reflecting what I felt in my heart. I'd lost so much more than just a husband when Billy died. I'd lost my purpose. The very thing I'd always wanted to do—and had done—but only for a short period of time.

Joe opened his mouth to speak, but before he could, one of the children eased up beside him and tugged on his shirt sleeve.

"What's up, Bernard?" Joe asked, the tone of his voice calm and coaxing.

"I'm thirsty, Papa Joe." The child—a rascal with a round face and dark eyes—smiled up at Joe.

Joe nodded, conceding. Our grown-up conversation was over. "I gotcha, big man."

Joe stood, scooping Bernard under one arm like a sack of potatoes. He ambled toward the back door, weaving once in his steps. I watched as his free hand hovered over his left side, fleetingly, as though he wanted to press into it but caught himself. He turned toward me again. "Don't go nowhere, now. We got a lot to catch up on."

I nodded but said nothing.

Joe opened the back screen door and set Bernard down. As the boy scurried in, Joe grasped the door's facing with a hand and squeezed.

"Yes, we do," I said, though I knew he couldn't hear me.

Chapter Seven

AFTER THE DOOR closed behind Joe and Bernard, I shifted on the bench to better watch the activity at the tables. Denise stood over one of the children, pointing to a workbook splayed before him and speaking gently. I couldn't make out the words, but her manner was encouraging, not only to this child but to all the kids.

Beyond them, on the last table, one lonely snow cone rested in its cardboard container. I thought of Keisha and of how Macon had taken most of the candy I'd meant for her. She'd looked so disappointed, though I had a hunch this was not unusual behavior from her older brother. In fact, I suspected that, to his way of thinking, the candy had been meant for him all along.

I walked past Denise and the studious children. Lifting the snow cone I said, "Hey, Denise? Tell Joe I'll be back in a little bit."

I didn't bother to ask if I could take the snow cone. I knew she and Joe wouldn't mind, especially if they knew where I was headed with it.

"Okay, baby," she said.

I walked the length of the ivy-laced fence, between the chain-link and the unpainted boards of the privacy fence, to a place big enough for anyone—child or adult—to pass through, to the front of the house and to the street where my car was parked. Mattie's apartment was only a couple of streets over, so within minutes I was back at the apartment building. This time I parked closer to where I now knew Macon and Keisha lived. When I stepped out of the car, snow cone in hand, I paused to observe a group of older age girls skipping rope, chanting and laughing. Watching them reminded me of the song I'd heard Joe and Denise sing with the children, making me wish I'd done or said something more than "uh."

I wondered why these girls were not a part of Joe's group. Age, perhaps? Had Joe and Denise not started what was obviously their mission here until recently? And if so, what happened to cause Joe to want to be a part of all this?

As I stepped around the corner of a building and came within earshot and eyesight of Macon and Keisha's home, I heard Macon's laughter. It reverberated through the common area and bounced between the lines of freshly washed clothes. Anthony's front storm door slammed open, hitting the wall and rattling the bars. I watched as Macon dashed out of the dark apartment, proudly sporting a man's red hoodie. It hung on his body two sizes too big as he performed an impromptu dance between their two buildings.

"Boy!"

I stepped back behind the corner of the apartment building, inching my head around the edge to see Anthony storming after Macon. He no longer wore his do-rag. His hair was neatly braided into short cornrows. A large tattoo stood prominent on the side of his neck, something I hadn't noticed before. He wore only a muscle tee, his work pants, and boots.

Macon turned to look at the man he obviously admired, though I couldn't imagine why. "Yo, yo!" Macon chanted. "Check out the OG, holdin' it down out here! *Yeah!*"

Anthony strode toward Macon, grabbed him by the shoulders. He glanced in my direction, which caused me to duck behind the wall before peering again. Anthony jerked the hoodie from Macon's body. "Don't you *ever* let me catch you wearin' this again, you *hear* me?" He wadded the hoodie with his hands. Even from where I stood, I could see the veins bulging along his neck.

The hurt registering on Macon's face met head-on with the anger and indignation in Anthony's. I couldn't quite read T. Was this anger because Macon had gotten into his personal possessions? Or was it like that of a father trying to raise his son not to cross some line, some boundary? Clearly the red hoodie was more than just any piece of clothing. This one, I began to see, tied the young men in this neighborhood together.

"Man, what's *wrong* witchu?" Macon's voice rose an octave higher than usual. "I was just playing!" He was wounded, not by Anthony's force so much, but by his displeasure. Anyone could see that.

"Go home, Macon!"

"Man, I'm sorry, all right?" The words echoed between the buildings.

Anthony turned, and I stepped out of view one more time, but only for a second. When I looked again, Macon stood dejected, arms extended at half mast by his sides, clearly wondering what he'd done wrong.

My breath came quickly as Anthony glanced around, searching for any witnesses to the moment. I did the same, but the few people who were in the common area just didn't seem to notice.

Anthony's eyes ran past where I stood behind the brick wall, undetected. I was grateful that I had not arrived a minute or even a second earlier, that I had stopped long enough to watch the girls skipping rope.

"Boy, *git* inside that house," Anthony said, pointing to Macon's door before storming into his own.

I took another breath, rested my head against the brick wall, and stared straight ahead to the side of the next building, no different from this one. It was then I realized my hand was wet and sticky. I looked down. The cup holding the snow cone had been crushed. Red slush dripped over my fist and onto the dead grass below.

I DIDN'T RETURN to Joe's. I decided I'd call him later. I had something important to do, and when I told him about it—if I told him about it—I was sure he would understand.

I drove straight home and much too fast. Once there, I ran inside and made a beeline for the upstairs office where I kept the file that held everything to do with Billy's murder. Every newspaper article. Every card from the officers, detectives, and hospital staff. Every note I'd made while talking to one of them on the phone.

I flipped the top of the file open and shifted papers around until I found the business card I needed. Signs of the rain from that night hadn't faded—the card was torn in a couple of places, puckered in others. But the information was still easy to read:

DECTECTIVE BRENT MILLER, HOMICIDE
METRO NASHVILLE POLICE DEPARTMENT
DIRECT LINE: (615) 555-7206

I dialed the number, but it went to voice mail. I hung up without leaving a message. I then pulled a phone book from a drawer and dropped it unceremoniously on top of a scattering of bills and past-due notices I hadn't cared enough lately to deal with. Dust whooshed up from the surrounding desk. I located the address for the police department, all the while wondering why the detective didn't have it on his card. Perhaps he liked a game of cat-and-mouse. If he did, I was in luck. I tried three pens before I found one with enough ink, and I jotted the address on the back of the card.

I grabbed a knee-length hooded sweater from my bedroom closet, then ran down the stairs to the kitchen. There I grabbed the keys to the truck from the key-shaped wooden holder Billy had crafted and hung next to the sink. I replaced them with the keys to my car.

The needle on my car's gas gauge was edging dangerously near "E," but more importantly, I wanted—no, I *needed*—to be as close to my husband as possible right now. To smell what little bit of his scent was left there. To picture him sitting beside me as

I drove down the now darkening country road toward the neon lights and skyscrapers of Nashville.

Locating the block of government offices wasn't difficult, but finding a decent parking place was. I drove up one level of the municipal parking garage after another until, frustrated, I found a space that wasn't marked "Reserved." Nervous tingles ran up my spine as I walked to the elevator. The heels of my western boots echoed in the cavernous garage, which only added to the ominous feeling I'd had since watching the encounter between Macon and Anthony.

It had been nearly three years since I'd been inside the police station, and I'd never been to Detective Miller's office. During the investigation into Billy's murder, he'd always met me at my home or at a downtown coffee shop. The first couple of times was to share with me what the police knew about the killer—the red hoodie, the mechanic's rag. The final time was to say the case had gone cold. That there were no further leads. Nothing concrete to tie any one person to the man who'd shot my husband. Who'd taken away my life.

But now, I may have uncovered something. I could feel it in my bones. Now all I had to do was convince someone in authority.

Detective Miller's office was located on the second floor, where the odor of stale coffee and smoked cigars lingered like the smell of dirty socks in a laundry hamper. I approached a female officer behind a tall counter where she stood slipping pink pieces of paper into case files.

"Can I help you?" she said without looking up.

"I'm hoping . . ." I cleared my throat. "I'm hoping Detective Brent Miller is in this evening."

She looked up. One eyebrow arched quizzically. "Miller?"

"Yes."

"You're in luck. He walked back in not ten minutes ago."

I wrapped my fingers around the straps of my purse and squeezed. "Could you tell him Samantha Crawford is here, please?"

"Will he know what this is about?"

"I think so, but . . . if not, you could tell him I'm Billy Crawford's wife." It felt odd—*good*—using the title again. "My husband was killed down in the Commons about three years ago and I—"

The officer closed the top of one of the folders, added it to a stack leaning against the corner of her work station. "Three years ago?"

I cleared my throat again. "Detective Miller worked the case, and I think I might have some information."

"Mm, okay." She pointed to a spot behind me. "Just have a seat over there, and I'll get him."

I sat down in the waiting area. Across from me were two adults—one male, one female. They clutched each other's hands and looked anxious. The knees of the woman bobbed up and down. She muttered, "I cannot *believe* she's gotten herself into this mess. Never in my life . . . No one—do you hear me?—*no one* in my family has *ever* been arrested."

To which the man replied, "Just hold on. We don't know anything yet."

I glanced to my right. A young man no more than twenty or twenty-one slouched in a chair, head dropped into his hand. Shaggy blond hair fell over his face. His breathing indicated he was asleep, as if he'd been there so long he'd finally given up and nodded off. I wondered if I should have called the front desk for an appointment after my failed attempt to reach Detective Miller directly.

But moments later I heard my name. Looking past the still-sleeping young man, I saw the man I remembered from three years ago. He hadn't changed much. Still slightly overweight, his silver hair combed back in a Conway Twitty style, though not quite as thick as it had been. His clothing hadn't changed all that much either. He still wore dress pants, white dress shirt, simple sports coat, and a tie.

I stood. "Hi. Detective Miller, I was wondering if I might have a minute of your time?"

For a moment I thought I saw annoyance register in his eyes. But just as quickly, it changed to compassion. He looked at his watch before saying, "I've got some time, sure. Come on back to my office."

I followed him, past the high counter, through makeshift offices that had been formed in the corners along the wide hallways. Detective Miller stepped aside as we neared the opaque glass door where his name and title had been professionally painted. I couldn't help but think of how different the letters looked from the ones on Joe's mailbox.

"Come in," he said.

The office was small. One wall was brick and glass, the windows looking out at the well-lit, white-brick courthouse that stood proudly behind the lawns of the public square. A nondescript office desk dominated the middle of the room. Two office chairs were in front of it, plaques and framed certificates mounted on the wall behind it. A coffee mug filled with pens and handheld flags from various police organizations stood at the top right-hand corner of the desk. On the left was a file tray neatly filled with manila folders and a flip-top Landscapes of America calendar. In the center was a chrome desk lamp, which cast the only light in the room other than that which came from the out-side. Detective Miller was obviously a man of order, which was good. I needed him to see—to understand—what I now knew. If it made sense in my mind, then surely it would in his.

I walked to a chair but didn't sit, choosing to remain standing with my hands clasped together.

Detective Miller strolled to the other side of his desk. I noticed he still walked with a limp. "Please, sit."

I did, dropping my purse to the floor. "Detective Miller," I said, my voice barely audible. "I was down in the projects today—the Commons—and I think I may have found something . . . someone . . . linked to my husband's—to Billy's murder."

Detective Miller chose, for whatever reason, to remain stand-ing. "What in the world was someone like you doing down there, Ms. Crawford?" The tone of his voice was gentle. Fatherly. Not as Anthony's had been earlier to Macon, but what I would have expected from my own sweet dad had I told him where I'd been that day.

Or the night before.

"I was checking on a couple of kids I helped get to the ER—"

"Oh, yeah, yeah, yeah. The hit-and-run last night. Girl from the projects. I heard about that. Happened near Murphy's. That right?"

I nodded. "Mm. Yes. Well . . . while I was in the Commons, I saw this guy. He matched your description of Billy's killer."

Detective Miller folded his arms over his chest. "I don't remember giving a description."

"Maybe 'description' isn't the right word. What I meant was . . . this guy had a red hoodie. And I'm pretty sure he's a mechanic. He, um . . . he had a red mechanic's rag."

The detective looked toward the ceiling briefly before his eyes came back to mine. He pressed his palms onto the top of his desk and leaned forward. "So you're a detective now? You do understand we questioned every mechanic and chop shop operator in a five-mile grid."

I wasn't about to tell him how to do his job any more than I would have expected him to tell me how to write a children's book, but I had to make him understand. At the very least, to know what I knew. "He had a red *hoodie*," I said again. *And a red mechanic's rag.*

Detective Miller shook his head. "Here's a news flash for you: All the bangers wear red hoodies down there."

I felt my breath catch in my throat.

The gentleness in the detective's eyes returned. "You're grasping at straws, Ms. Crawford."

"But . . ." I shook my head just enough to shake loose my own thoughts. I *couldn't* be grasping at straws. If that were the case, then chances were, Billy's killer would *never* be caught. Would never be brought to trial. He'd never serve time behind bars. At least, not for *this* crime. For *Billy's* murder.

Detective Miller arched his back so that he stood to his full height. He sighed deeply. "You have no idea, Ms. Crawford, how many investigations are ongoing in that neighborhood. Yours isn't the only one. And I'm sorry to say, nothing much really gets solved out there." He sighed again as he shoved his hands into his pants pockets. "Look. I'm no racist, but I *am* a realist." He glanced over his shoulder to the window and the world outside it. "We're talking about the *Commons.* They throw a party if a boy makes his twenty-first birthday because he's defying the odds."

My heart hurt. I thought of Macon. Of the boys I'd met today—Snuffy and Bernard and the others—of their smiling faces and how, if what Detective Miller had just said was true, these boys may never reach adulthood. Simply because of where they lived.

Detective Miller rolled his chair around to the side of the desk nearest to me. He sat, rested his elbows on his knees, and looked me in the eye with as much compassion, I suppose, as a man could who'd put in the same length of time in his line of work. "Did you ever play with pit bull pups, Ms. Crawford?" I could smell tobacco and mint gum on his breath. "So cute and cuddly." His brow creased. "But then they grow up. And they become what nature intended them to be." He shook his head. "They can't help it." He looked out the window again. "I think about those kids you picked up . . . and I wonder." His eyes, sad and washed out with disappointment, returned again to mine. "What might they become someday? If they make it."

I could hear my own breathing, could feel my heart pounding in my chest. I reached toward the floor without taking my eyes off his, stretching my fingers until they found the strap of my purse. I drew it up, clutched it to my roiling stomach.

I hadn't eaten all day. But more than that, this meeting had left me nauseated.

"Ms. Crawford . . . you've lost so much. I know. And I'm sorry. But you stand to lose a lot more if you keep going into the Commons. For *any* reason. Trust me." One brow rose. "Take solace in this fact: The man who killed your husband? He's probably already dead."

The air left my lungs. I stood. Numbness overwhelmed me. At the same time, a new sort of anger coursed through me. "Thank you for your time, Detective."

I turned toward the door. I willed my legs and my feet to move forward, keeping my focus on the corridor before me. After I passed the chairs where the man continued to sleep and the couple continued to lament, I began to walk faster, more determined than I'd been when I'd walked in.

More so than I'd even been last night.

If Detective Miller couldn't find the man who killed my husband, then I would.

Chapter Eight

I IMMEDIATELY RETURNED to the Commons, rolling Billy's truck to a stop at a darkened curb, positioning myself between two of the buildings. I killed the engine, huddled down in the seat, and pulled the hood of my green sweater over my head. Raking my teeth over my lower lip, I turned my head toward Anthony's apartment. There, beneath the streetlamp, I could see three mechanic's rags hanging on a wire that had been tied between one of the bars on the front window and a porch post. Two were white.

One was red.

My eyes wandered left to where Mattie sat in the shadows beside her front door. The crimson glow of a cigarette singed in the cold air. Her porch light wasn't on, but I could see the outline of her face whenever she drew on the cigarette. She looked older and more tired than she had even this morning. After one more draw, she flicked the cigarette into the air. It landed in the grass a few feet away, and within seconds it had burned out. With that, Mattie stood and staggered to her front door and into the dark apartment.

The sound of breaking glass caused me to look out the other window. Across the street four black men sat in folding lawn chairs around a makeshift bonfire built in the rusty remains of a patio grill. They all held cans of beer or bottles hidden in brown paper bags. Just like Mattie's.

These men were already drunk. Past drunk. Unable to sit up straight. Laughing at . . . nothing. Could one of these men have been Billy's killer? And while he lay cold in his grave, was his murderer sitting around a warm fire, laughing and drinking as though life was just peachy? As though nothing in the world was wrong?

Or was I right in my suspicions about Anthony? This man Macon and Mattie called T. I'd seen his anger. He'd been mad enough earlier today to do something murderous. But what would Billy have done—*could* Billy have done—to infuriate Anthony to the point of murdering him? Billy's wallet had been left beside him, and nothing was missing from it. If robbery wasn't the motive, if the attack hadn't been provoked and brought on by anger, then what could have caused someone to murder my husband? Or could it have been random, as Detective Miller once suggested to me?

I sat up, cut my eyes over at Anthony's front door once more. Somehow I had to get inside that apartment. I had to see for myself what Detective Miller refused to look into.

And I would. Somehow.

I swallowed hard, started up the truck, and drove home.

WITH THE EXCEPTION of a few trips to the barn to care for the horses and other animals, I stayed in bed the entire weekend, nearly unable to move. Unable to think. Unable to eat more than a few bites of food. Unable to do anything but sleep, covers pulled high over my head. I dreamed about Billy. About red hoodies and red rags and red blood spilling onto the street.

Sometimes I dreamed of fires and men sitting around them, laughing and drinking.

Other times I dreamed of the campfire Billy had built shortly before he died. I could see his hand clutching a pine branch, poking at the embers, stoking the fire. Stirring up my love for him with every breath we breathed together.

In one dream I read to him my story about little Firebird and, when it was done, he leaned back and kissed me. The moment was so real, I could taste him. Smell him. I woke feeling magical, as though the dream had been real. And when I realized it was not, that such a moment would never happen again, I cried so hard, my sobs forced me out of bed. To the bathroom, where I vomited into the toilet before returning to bed.

A few days later I managed to drag myself to the shower. I dressed. I ate a bowl of cereal. I went to the barn, spent time feeding and talking to the livestock, and took a short ride on Cricket. Another one on Penny. After un-tacking both, I got in the car and drove back into the city. Back to Joe's to tell him I was sorry for the way I'd walked out on him without explanation.

I knocked on his door, but no one answered. When I heard the sound of children's laughter coming from the backyard, I strolled past the side of the house to where Joe's children sat on patches of the grassy walkway between flower beds. He sat on a table's bench, elbows on his knees, gazing lovingly toward the kids. Beside him, a child's bright-yellow beach pail was filled with bags of M&Ms and other candies.

I smiled at seeing them. At seeing Keisha and Macon in the group. And at Denise, who sat at the edge of the group with Bernard tucked into her lap.

"All right," Joe said, drawing excitement with his words. "What time is it?"

"Joe's Honor Roll!" the children shouted in unison.

"Excellent work this time around, guys. I'm really, really proud of you. I will be posting your names in the Commons so everyone can see just how great you all are." He pulled a bag of M&Ms from the pail. "First up, the man who flat-out rocked it. A man who came up in four classes." He held up the corresponding number of fingers. "*Snuffy*," he said, saying the name as though he were Louie Armstrong singing in a jazz club.

Snuffy stood as the others clapped. He made his way through the small crowd, hugged Joe, and took his candy.

Joe kept going, "Bernard . . . Peach . . . Chloe . . ." He handed each child a small bag of candy. "Keisha . . ."

My heart flipped at hearing Keisha's name, at seeing her—with only the smallest of bandages now—stand to claim her prize.

"Snoop . . . Trent . . . and Willis." As each name was called, another child stood to proudly claim his or her reward.

"Ex-cell-ent work." Joe looked into the near-empty pail. "Man, you guys are emptying the bucket here. Make a hungry man cry." He clapped. "Great job, guys."

Macon stood from the crowd. He looked handsome in an oversized green and white argyle sweater worn over a long-sleeved blue tee, and a pair of dark denim jeans. He approached Joe, who met him with eyes intent on yielding all of his attention to the child.

I took a few steps closer, to hear what Macon had to say, realizing then he'd been the only one not called up for candy.

"You owe me some of that."

Joe seemed to swallow back a smile. "Oh really. Enlighten me."

Macon looked at the others, making sure they were engrossed in their own bags of candy. "Five *A*'s, baby."

"Is that right?"

"Yes, sir."

"Never saw any proof, Einstein."

"'Cause I don't want my name up on that board."

"And why is that?"

"I got my reasons."

"Well, I'm sure you do. But until I see that card, and you let me post your name, I'm gonna assume you doin' what you do best. Which is puttin' the hustle on me."

Macon's head wove side to side. "I ain't hustlin' you, man."

Joe's eyes grew large. "Then bring me your card, playa." He fisted his hand, gave Macon a love tap on his chest. "Show me what you made of."

Macon turned, tsk-ing, frustration etched on his face. "This is stupid, man."

I bit my lip to keep from laughing. It appeared Joe was doing the same. But beyond the smile, the look he gave Macon showed just how much he cared. How much he *loved* this boy who was "one of his kids," but wasn't.

Joe leaned back, resting his elbows on the table. When he did, he spotted me standing close by. "Well, well!" he said. The children stopped chattering, looked at Joe, and followed his gaze to me. "She lives!"

I smiled, my whole body filled with warmth, the first fragment of warmth I'd felt in days. Before that . . . years. Even riding the horses today hadn't given me this feeling.

"Hey, kids," Joe said, bringing their attention back to him. "Y'all got time for a quick story?"

A cheer rose from the small group.

"See that woman right there?" He nodded toward me.

The children nodded, and Denise smiled at me.

"She saved my life once. When we were kids."

Oh, no. He wouldn't . . .

"Y'all wanna hear about it?"

I shook my head, but the kids cheered again. "Yeah!"

Joe pressed his fingers to his lips. "Shh . . . listen now. It was on a Saturday," he began, "not too many months after I first met Miss Sam. I was walking through these woods that we used to play in all the time. A wonderful place for thinking, for being alone, and for being with your best friend." Joe looked up at me, winked, and turned back to the children. "Now, Miss Sam there, she was always drawing pictures on this sketch pad and making up stories about whatever she drew. I happened to be walking through the woods on this particular Saturday when I spied her, sitting with her back against a tree, drawing. I also happened to see a pretty bird perched up on an old tree stump, posing for little Miss Sam."

The children looked back at me and giggled.

"Well," Joe continued, drawing their attention back to him. "I snuck around the tree—it was a big oak tree—and . . . 'Hiiiiiiii-yaaaaa-hhhh!'" Joe jumped toward the children, landing in a karate-chop pose.

I had walked over to sit next to Joe by now, granting me a full view of the kids. Their eyes grew large as they jerked in place at Joe's theatrics. The look on Denise's face told me she'd already heard this story.

"The little bird flew away," Joe said, casting his eyes upward as though that very same bird were here now, then gone.

"Little Sam said, 'You scared away my bird friend.'"

The children giggled again, this time at Joe's voice, made high and squeaky to imitate mine at that age. "She turned her drawing pad toward me and, sure enough, there it was, that same little bird, drawn just as pretty and perfect as you please. But Miss Sam was not happy with me. No, she was not. She said, 'He was the main character in my new story. See?'

"'Oh, yeah? What's this one about?' I asked her.

"She said, 'It's about this little bird who finds out God even cares for the little sparrows. Then he's happy.'

"'That's it?' I asked her. 'Why you always messin' with all that drawing and story-tellin' stuff?'

"Now, what I haven't told you is about what I was wearing at the time. I had on this really cool karate gi—a uniform, let's call it—but I just wore the top, not the bottoms. My grandmother had bought it for me at a thrift store." He nodded at the kids, knowing they understood. "So there I was wearing my gi, white sash all tied around my waist, a pair of cutoff jeans, and a makeshift black cape. I am telling you right now, I . . . looked . . . cool."

I breathed out a sigh and a smile, hoping the children couldn't tell from my own memory of the event just how uncool he'd been. But they saw, all right, and they giggled.

Joe looked at me. "Stay out of this," he teased. "Today, I'm the storyteller."

I sat up straight and saluted him. Denise laughed silently.

"May I continue?" he asked his audience.

"Yeah!"

"So Miss Sam says, 'Why are you always wearing your pajamas in public?'

"'For the *last time*,' I said, 'these are *not* pajamas!' This only made Little Sam giggle. But she was my best friend, so I couldn't be mad at her, now could I?"

"Nooooooo," they said.

"I took her by the hand and said, 'Come with me.' We walked for a ways, and then I made Miss Sam cover her eyes." He briefly covered his eyes, and I did the same, showing the children how agreeable I'd been so many years before. "I told her, 'We're going somewhere special.' And then I took her to my secret place. I'd gotten some old metal and boards and made a lean-to. I also got one of my grandmother's potato sacks and filled it with pine straw, hung it up, and used it as a punching bag."

Joe fisted his hands and boxed the air around him.

"I got an old pair of my grandpa's pants and a hoodie and filled those full of straw too. Propped them up on a stick like a scarecrow." He boxed the air again. "All the bad people in the world was inside that one scarecrow, and I was the hero to be reckoned with.

"I told Little Sam, 'I'm going to be a samurai warrior one day.' I picked up this tin bucket I'd brought from home, put it on my head, and gave her my best samurai pose." Joe stretched his upper torso to its full height, placed his fists on his hips, and swung from side to side.

I looked at the children. He had them mesmerized.

"Miss Sam reminded me there were no black samurai warriors. Can you believe that? I just said, 'I know. But I'm one of a kind!' I then showed her how tough I was by grabbing hold of this stick I'd nailed between two posts—a chin-up bar for making me strong." Joe demonstrated his actions, fists clutched in the air, pulled his chin to the bar, back down, back up, back down.

I shook my head. "If I remember correctly," I said, "you got your nose to the bar, but your chin never made it."

Joe looked at me, pretending to be put out. "Who's telling this story?"

I smiled at the children. "Please, continue then."

"Okay, so it's true. I wasn't very strong in those days. But I had a plan, you see. I said, 'I'm gonna train hard, fight hard. Gonna get out of this little town. Live in the big city. Save the world! I'm gonna be big, Sam. *Huge*.' And do you know what she said?"

"Nooooooo."

I decided to answer the question. With a half smile I said, "'Writing stories is still way cooler.'"

"What did Papa Joe say to that?" Bernard asked.

"He said, 'Whatever.'"

"I decided to show Sam what I was made of," Joe went on. "'Oh, you ain't seen nothin' yet,' I told her. I boxed at the potato sack a few times and then front-kicked the legs right out from under that scarecrow." Joe leaned forward. "What I didn't know, was I had just disturbed the hiding place of a big ol' rattlesnake."

The kids drew back.

"That thing shook its rattles at me. Hissin'. Little Sam gasped like a girl, but I was Samurai Joe. 'Stay back, Sam,' I told her. 'I got this.' I grabbed a broomstick I had propped up nearby, never taking my eyes off that viper. I twirled the stick slowly, slowly like a Japanese fighting bo . . ." Joe continued making the motions as the children leaned toward their storyteller. "Miss Sam was scared, but not me. Not Samurai Joe. I wasn't backin' down. I jabbed at the snake . . . jab . . . jab . . . when . . . whoosh!" Joe lunged at the children. They screamed. Even I jumped a little.

"That snake bit me right on the leg." He nodded toward me. "Little Sam here had to tote me all the way back home. She carried me, dragging my body through the woods, blood dripping down my leg, until I passed out cold in the grass."

"Then what happened?" Snuffy asked.

"I ran as fast as I could to get help," I said. "The ambulance came and took Joe to the hospital where . . . he got better." I didn't say the rest. I didn't tell them how I'd begged my daddy to take me to the hospital to see Joe that evening. I didn't say how I'd seen his grandmother sitting next to the bed where he lay, reading from her Bible. I'd never even told Joe what I'd heard from where I'd paused just outside the door. About how he'd asked his grandmother if his father was coming.

"No, baby," she answered. "I called him, but he . . . he ain't gonna be able to make it."

Joe nodded as though he understood. Then he asked, "Grandma, am I gonna die?"

Joe's grandmother shook her head. "I don't think the good Lord's done with you jus' yet. I think you got a long life ahead of you, boy."

"Grandma?"

"Yes, sir?"

"How come my dad don't love me?"

I remember how my heart hurt at such a question. I'd never known such sorrow. My father had shown me nothing but love my whole life. All I wanted in that moment was to run into the room, to throw my arms around my young friend and tell him how much I loved him.

Joe's grandmother saw me then. Her face grew bright, and she smiled. "Well, look-a here. Look at this pretty thing." She turned to Joe. "You got yourself a visitor."

"Hi," I said, stepping into the small hospital room.

"Come on over here, Miss," his grandmother said, closing her Bible and placing it on the bedside table.

I stepped over to the bed and peered at Joe, who looked pitiful with his half-opened eyes, dry and cracking lips, and oxygen tubes up his nose. I pulled a piece of paper out of the sketch pad I carried and handed it to him. "Made you somethin'," I said. It was the *Samori Joe* sketch he now kept framed and hanging in his hallway.

"Samurai Joe," Joe had muttered, his dark hair looking all the darker against the white pillowcase. "Yeah. That's what I'm talking about." He looked back at his grandmother with a set jaw. "I was thinking . . . you survive a snakebite, you can survive just about anything. I mean, you're invincible. And you're strong enough to make it on your own."

Grandma sighed before looking straight into her grandson's eyes. "No, baby. Ain't none of us that strong. And you ain't got to be. 'Cause you never really on your own, Joe. You're never alone."

With just over a dozen children sitting at our feet, Joe now looked at me and I at him. He reached his hand toward mine that night, just as he was doing now. And, as before, I slipped mine into his.

"Truth is," Joe said to the children sitting before us, "I would have died that day if Sam hadn't been there with me." He squeezed my hand before releasing it. "Now, how many of you guys comin' up without a father?" he asked them, causing me to wonder if he remembered the part of the story neither of us seemed willing to share.

Most of their hands slid upward, which took my breath away.

"Yeah," Joe said. "It's tough sometimes. I know. But there's one thing my grandma told me that day. Sometimes life is cruel.

Makes you sad or angry, maybe even want to hurt somebody. But no matter how hard life gets . . ."

Joe swallowed hard, and tears swam in his eyes. He looked first at me, then back to the kids. "No matter how hard life is . . . you're *never* alone."

Chapter Nine

THE MOOD HAD grown too somber—it was too much for me. For the children. Even Denise seemed at a loss for what to do or say next.

Then Joe clapped his hands in a cadence. The children and Denise followed his lead, clapping the same rhythm. When they were done, Joe smiled. "All right. I got some good news, and I got some bad news."

The children cried out, "Bad news first!"

"The bad news is: Food truck's not comin' tomorrow." He stood, walked around the gathering of children whose faces showed more than just disappointment. It was as if a lifeline had been snatched out of their hands. "The good news is . . ." By now Joe had reached the back porch where a large green tarp was laid over what appeared to be a small angular mountain. He pulled the tarp away, revealing stacked boxes filled with nonperishable foods. *"It's already here!"*

The kids jumped from their places and ran to the porch. Joe handed each child a box, one at a time, speaking to them individually before adding to the whole, "Hurry up! PB&J when you get back!"

Keisha and Macon stood at the back of the line. Denise walked with the first recipients toward the back gate—the hole in the fence I'd walked through last week. I joined Joe and stood close enough to ask, "How are you doing all this, Joe?"

He seemed humbled by the question. "It's amazing what happens if you just ask." I watched his eyes wander across the yard to where Denise stood watching the backs of the children as they headed home with their treasure. "Actually, my neighbor Denise came up with this whole thing. I'm just . . ." He pressed his lips together. Shook his head. "I'm just doing my part."

Macon and Keisha had made it to the front of the line. Joe handed them their box. They walked away, only making it to the swing set against the back fence where they stopped, placed the box on the ground, and stood. Joe motioned for me to sit again at the table, and I did.

"Hey," I said. "I'm . . . I'm sorry I disappeared on you."

"I'm sure you had your reasons," he said, sitting beside me.

I looked at Keisha and Macon, wondering what had made them stop. Keisha scribbled a note on her pad and showed it to her brother.

"Why doesn't she talk?" I asked Joe.

He sighed. "She used to, but she . . ." He turned his head so I would be the only one who could hear his words. "She's been through quite a lot."

"Joe? Can I ask you a question?"

"Sure."

"The other day I heard . . . someone . . . say something, and I don't know what it means."

"All right. You think I might be able to help you?"

"Yeah." I looked back at Macon and Keisha. The other children, who'd left minutes before, slowly returned to the yard. Two of the older girls sat at one of the tables and started talking with each other. Three of the younger children ran to the swing set.

I turned back to Joe. "This thing that I heard . . . it was like a song. Or a chant."

Joe's brows came together. "All right."

"It went, 'Check out the OG.' I don't know what that means."

"Who'd you hear say that?"

"Oh, just some kids over in the Commons." The truth was, I wanted to know if there was any connection between what Macon had been saying while wearing the red hoodie and what Detective Miller had said about all the bangers wearing them.

"It means the 'original gangster.'" He shook his head. "Most of the kids around here think that being a part of a gang is somehow cool. They don't get what it really means. That's why Denise and I are working so hard trying to make a difference."

I looked back at Macon again, wondering again why he and Keisha had been out so late the night of the accident. Why he chose to hang out with someone like Anthony. And why, when Joe called his honor roll, he alone was left without a sweet reward.

My gaze shifted to Keisha. She remained next to her brother, silent. I smiled, and when I did, she waved her hand, coaxing me to come to her.

Joe smiled. "She wants you to come along."

"To come along?"

"To take their food box home. That's probably what she's been waitin' on. You and me to be done with our talk. Keisha's respectful like that."

I nodded. "Okay." I stood and said to Joe, "We'll be back soon."

I could have driven, but I decided it was too nice a day to spend in the car. Macon was none too happy, but Keisha seemed pleased just to be with me. We walked back toward the Commons, me lugging the box of groceries and Macon talking a lot of "tough stuff." Keisha remained silent.

"So," Macon said with swagger, "where is it?"

"What? Where is what?"

He looked at me as though I'd lost my mind. "You still owe me a quarter."

I gave him the most incredulous look I could muster. "You're serious?"

Macon did nothing more than huff at me. He walked a few paces ahead to show his displeasure.

I sighed. If Macon were half as tough as he thought he was . . .

Keisha tugged on my sweater. I looked down at her. She had pulled a sketch pad from her backpack and flipped it open to one of the pages. Keisha had drawn a beautiful horse in colors of brown, black, and cream.

I stopped walking. "Wow, Keisha. Did you draw that?"

She nodded.

"That is an *amazing* drawing." I looked at Macon, who'd rejoined us. "We've got us a little artist here, Macon."

Macon acted unimpressed. "She's always drawing them dumb things."

"There's nothing dumb about a horse, now, Macon. They're the most amazing animals." I looked at Keisha. "Your drawing looks just like my horse, Cricket."

"Stupid waste-a time, if you ask me," Macon continued.

Keisha's eyes turned sad. She folded the cover of the sketch pad back over the drawing.

Furious, I turned back to Macon. "Well, no one asked you," I said before placing my hand under Keisha's chin and turning her face upward to look at me. "I think it's beautiful."

She smiled.

We continued on, past a large green Dumpster, where someone had recently tossed out several stained mattresses. In the warm autumn air, the odor of household garbage met us without apology. Macon and Keisha didn't seem to notice at all.

Just past the Dumpster, we were in sight of Macon and Keisha's apartment. I looked to the right, toward Anthony's. His front door was ajar. The mechanic's rags remained tossed over the wire along with a pair of blue Dickies. I stopped short, staring. Thinking.

"I don't think that's a good idea."

I was startled back to the children standing in front of me. "What?"

Keisha held up her notepad. Macon read it, shaking his head. He looked at me. "She wants you to come inside. I *don't* think it's a good idea."

"You want me to come inside?" I asked.

"She wants you to see her room. She's got lots of them drawings in there."

"You'll have to go ask your grandma if it's okay."

"She gonna say no," Macon said. "She don't like *white* people in her house."

"Wha—?"

Macon smiled. "Naw, I'm just playin'. I'll go see." He took Keisha by the hand. "Come on, Keisha."

Keisha walked alongside her brother, turned to look over her shoulder, and smiled at me. I returned the gesture.

Once they'd gone inside I looked around to see if anyone might be watching me. No one was.

I walked over to Anthony's front stoop and peered into the slightly opened door. "Hello?" I called.

No one answered.

I eased the door open with my foot, inched forward until I stood in the semidark foyer of the apartment. If he *was* there, I'd politely tell him he'd left his door open. It would be a plausible excuse. If he didn't . . .

A flight of shoe-scuffed stairs were directly in front of me, leading to a second floor. To the right was a small living room. Dingy. Paint chipping off the walls. The smell of motor oil and smoked cigars hung heavy in the air.

A portable television was near the doorway, sitting on top of two old fruit crates. On top of it was a DVD player and on top of that, a short stack of mail. I wanted to look through it, to learn as much as I could about this man named Anthony. This mechanic who owned a red hoodie and wiped grease from his hands with a red rag. I realized then that I still held the box of food in my arms. I set it down on the bottom stair, picked up the mail, and sorted through the envelopes.

All were addressed to Anthony Jones, 578 Shelby Avenue, Nashville.

I looked over my shoulder to the door and out to the common area. No one lurked nearby. The open door was surely providential. I decided to venture further into the apartment.

I peered down a hallway off from the living room, which led to an open back door. Only a buckling screen kept the flies out.

I moved down the hall, my heart beating like a stallion's. Fear pulled at me to stop, but I couldn't.

The first doorway on the left was a bedroom. It was as dark and foreboding as the living room. The windows were covered by a thin blue sheet stretched across tattered blinds and held up by thumbtacks. A mattress lay on the floor in one corner, disheveled linens and a blanket strewn across it.

A single lamp, left burning, illuminated a scarred dresser. I walked over to it. The floor creaked beneath my feet as I stopped and noted the items on top. A digital clock. A belt, rolled into a neat circle. A cheap plastic ashtray—the kind one finds on a café tabletop—with only the tip of a Black & Mild cigar and a few ashes.

I drew in a deep breath. From outside the window came the sound of children playing. Macon and Keisha would be looking for me soon, if not already. I had to hurry.

I slid open the top drawer of the dresser. Inside were several newspaper clippings. I removed them, flipping through each one.

WOMAN BURNED TO DEATH IN DRUG-RELATED FIRE, the first headline read. Another read 21-YEAR-OLD KILLED IN GANG SHOOTING.

One after the other, pictures of young black men stared back at me, each one dead. Killed by gang warfare. Violence. What was it Detective Miller had said to me? *This is the Commons. They throw a party if a boy makes his twenty-first birthday because he's defying the odds.*

What was this obsession Anthony Jones had with gang warfare?

My breath became ragged. I returned the clippings. As I did, I spied a wooden cigar box toward the back of the drawer. I slid the drawer farther open, retrieved it from the shadows, and set it carefully on top of the dresser.

I pressed my thumbs under the lid to open it, but just as I did, I heard the front storm door creak as it was being opened. Nerves prickled my body, starting at the top of my head and rushing down my spine. Fear coursed through my veins. I turned quickly, dashed into the hallway, and out the back door.

The squeaking of the screen as it opened, shut, and slammed behind me would surely give away my presence in Anthony's home. Frantic, I ran the length of Macon and Keisha's building, then up the side, past the electric meters, to the drainpipe running down the front edge as quickly as my boots would allow.

I heard Anthony slam out of his front door. "*Macon!*"

I leaned forward to look into the common area. Macon and Keisha stood where they had left me, looking perplexed. They'd both turned at hearing Anthony call Macon's name with such force and anger.

"I told you not to come in my house!" He pointed at Macon. "We gonna have to have a talk, boy!"

"What?" Macon asked, his voice squeaking defensively.

I took deep breaths, in through my nose, out my mouth, in an attempt to return my heartbeat to normal.

"You hear me?"

When Anthony's front door slammed shut, I darted toward the children, extending my hand to Keisha. "C'mon. Walk with me."

Keisha readily took my hand, keeping pace as I hurried back toward Joe's house.

"Wait up," Macon said, sounding authoritative. "What were you just doing?"

I shook my head, still barely able to breathe. "Just making friends. Now, let's go!"

Macon jumped in front of me, forcing me to stop. "You were in T's house." It wasn't a question.

"No, I wasn't."

"Aww, man! And you gave away our food!"

I looked down at my hands, felt my shoulders slump forward. Lord help me, I'd left the box in the foyer. I turned toward Anthony's apartment building, expecting him to be standing there, holding the box, ready to come after all of us. But the door was shut. There was no sign of T.

I looked back at Macon. "I'll get it back."

"How? How you gonna do that?"

"I mean I'll buy you more food. I'm good for it, Macon, so just let it go, okay?"

Keisha wrote on her notepad: ARE YOU OK?

I nodded. "I'm fine. I'll be fine."

We started walking again. I kept my eyes focused on the road ahead, which stretched left to right on the other side of the apartment buildings. If we could just get there, we'd be that much closer to Joe's. *Why hadn't I driven?*

"Naw, man," Macon continued. "I wanna know. What were you just doing?"

Who did this child think he was, asking an adult such questions? "Nothing."

"You the po-po." The police.

"Nope."

"FBI."

"No, Macon. This is ridiculous. I'm just a friend of Joe's, all right?"

"Naw, I'm not buyin' that. Give it to me straight, or I'm tellin' Joe you up to somethin'. I'll tell him you were in T's house."

I stopped again, this time facing him head on. I felt my face flush, my eyes grow narrow. "Oh, I see. Okay, I'll play along. Name your price."

"What?"

"Name your price. I've seen how you play. You want something from me. Am I right? So what's it gonna cost me, Macon? Name your price."

I watched his eyes shift back and forth as he calculated an answer. "Double what was in the grocery box. A case of Coke. Three big bags of M&Ms. And a roll of quarters."

"Is that all?"

Macon looked over to his sister, back to me. "The horse! You gonna take Keisha to see that horse of yours. And if you do one more crazy thing, I swear I'm telling Joe. I can promise you that."

I breathed a sigh of relief. Macon was a player all right. But he was straightforward with anyone who understood his rules. "Uh-hunh," I said, extending my hand toward him, daring him to shake it. "Well, sir. You just made me a promise."

Chapter Ten

I TOLD THE children to run on ahead of me and that I'd catch up to them. "Just get on back to Joe's," I said.

As soon as they were out of earshot, I pulled my phone from my purse. After meeting with Detective Miller the week before, I had entered his number into my phone in case I ever needed to speak with him again. Obviously, going to his office was a waste of time. But with what I now knew about Anthony Jones, there might be something more for him to look into.

I dialed the number, and it went straight to voicemail. "Detective Miller, this is Samantha Crawford. I know you think I'm crazy, but I need you to run a name for me. Anthony Jones. Five-seventy-eight Shelby Avenue, here in Nashville. He's a mechanic. Please. Just run the name and call me back." I recited my number before ending the call.

I flipped the top of my cell phone back into place just as a door squeaked open behind me. Anthony stepped out of the door and onto his stoop, no more than thirty yards away. He wore clean slacks and a pressed shirt. He pulled a cigarette from behind his ear. As he lit it, his eyes locked on where I stood, startling me. There was no mistaking it this time: He saw me.

I turned and walked, moving as quickly as I dared, forcing myself not to run so as not to appear afraid or out of place.

Quite honestly, I couldn't have been more of both.

BACK AT JOE'S, I found Macon sitting with Joe at one of the tables and having a private conversation. The noise of happy, playing children drowned out his words, but it was obvious Macon was telling on me.

Joe's look said it all.

He stood and confronted me. "Is this true?" Concern laced his words.

I closed my eyes momentarily, opening them to look at Macon with eyes of accusation.

"About the horse and the farm?" Joe said.

Denise stepped out of the back door, carrying a plate stacked with peanut-butter-and-jelly sandwiches. At seeing her, the kids rushed noisily for a seat at the picnic tables. I was grateful for the brief interruption, for the chance to look Macon in the eye, to see the mischief there. He was no deceiver—at least, not this time. This time he was a plotter.

"Oh," I said. "Yeah. Absolutely."

Joe's face showed nothing but gratitude. He clapped his hands. "Attention, ladies and gentlemen!"

The children stopped instantly, as did Denise. All gave their full attention to Papa Joe. "I got a huge announcement. Out of the graciousness of her heart, Miss Sam has invited all of you on a field trip to her farm!"

The children erupted in cheers of pleasure and excitement.

And what was I to say? I could only smile at them. At Denise, whose hand was now clasped over her mouth in surprise. At Joe, whose look of genuine appreciation was almost more than I could bear.

And at Macon, who gave me his best "I just got you so good" expression. I swallowed. He may be the child, and I may be the adult, but there was no doubt I'd have to get up earlier in the morning to keep up with him.

One of the older girls raised her hands. "Papa Joe?"

"Yeah, Peach?"

"When?"

Joe looked at me.

Today was Wednesday. Thursday and Friday were school days. If they came on Saturday, we could make it an overnighter. "Uh . . . Saturday?"

Joe clapped his hands once, before rubbing them together. "Saturday it is!"

Bernard raised his hand. "Papa Joe? How we all gonna get there?"

Joe blinked. He looked first to Denise, then to me. I certainly couldn't get everyone in my car, and it wasn't safe or legal to allow the children to ride in the back of Billy's truck. I shrugged.

Then Joe said, "No worries. Papa Joe is about to place a call to the best bus driver in Nashville!"

With that, the children cheered again.

BRICK MADE THE necessary calls to secure the school bus for the field trip to my home. Joe and Denise used the time to obtain permissions from the parents and guardians of the children, while I spent all of Thursday and Friday cleaning a farmhouse that had barely seen a dust cloth or a spritz of Windex since Billy died.

I got a call from Denise on Friday afternoon that everything was a go. We decided I'd drive to the city and leave my car at Joe's so I could ride with the children on the bus. This would allow me to point out various animals and locations to kids who'd never seen a farm animal in person—or a stretch of land that was not marked by cement and graffiti.

I arrived early on Saturday, helped Denise and Joe with last-minute arrangements, gathered permission slips from fifteen highly excited children, and then waited on the sidewalk as impatiently as they for Brick to show up. Finally, at about a quarter till nine, the long yellow bus lurched down the narrow, tree-lined street of Joe's neighborhood.

The kids jumped up and down—all except Keisha. She quietly sidled up to me and took my hand. I glanced into her lovely face—I thought a more beautiful angel could not be found anywhere—and smiled. Mattie had dressed her in jeans, a yellow sweater, and a denim over-shirt. Her hair was caught up in thick pigtails by ponytail holders with large yellow balls. Keisha was nothing short of wonder and color, and she looked at me with eyes of gratitude beyond any I'd seen before.

The moment shook me. In my mind this was just a two-day field trip to a farm. But to Keisha, it was a taste of something more than life had offered her so far. Whatever had happened to strike her silent, I didn't know. What I did know was that in the few short years of her childhood, she had never experienced the fairy tale world I had written books about. Had *always* written about, even as a child. Because that life was all I had ever known.

While Brick helped Joe load backpacks filled with clothes and toiletries, Denise and I counted heads as each child climbed onto the bus. "Take your seat, take your seats," she called, though there was really no need. These children were anxious to get where they were going.

Denise sat in a middle seat near the children. Joe sat behind Brick, who wore a brightly colored cowboy hat and seemed as excited as the children, if not more so. I sat across from Joe, close enough to the driver to give directions. Every so often I caught a glimpse of the wheeled medical apparatus I'd seen in Joe's bedroom, which was now wedged between him and the side of the bus. Periodically, he pushed it back into its place.

It wasn't my place to ask, but I couldn't help but wonder . . .

The children sang songs at first, but as the city gave way to rural stretches of land, they turned their attention to new surroundings, sticking their faces and arms out the opened windows.

"Coooooowwwwwwssss," they hollered when we drove alongside a pasture.

"Goooooooaaaaaattttssss!"

"What's that, Papa Joe?" Bernard hollered, pointing across the road.

"That's called a silo."

"A silo? What's a silo?"

Joe shook his head with a mixture of amusement and sorrow. He looked at me, his eyes saying, *How is it a kid doesn't know what a silo is?*

"It's a place for storing grain," Denise answered.

"Grrrrraaaaaiiiinnnnn!"

As we neared the road leading to my farm, I grew more anxious. No one had been here, really, since Billy died, other than the men who worked the farm, and my parents who came for an occasional visit to make sure their daughter hadn't curled up and died. But I hadn't *entertained* anyone, child or adult. Not that I expected the children would rate me on my hospitality skills. I did wonder how the children would see me once they saw where I lived. By Tennessee standards, it was an adequate stretch of farmland, though it barely broke even. But for these children who lived in little more than a thousand square feet of peeling paint, dark hallways, and secondhand furniture, my little farm would seem a paradise.

Joe and Denise lived and worked in their world; the children could identify with them. But would the kids think less of me after today? Would Joe or Denise?

But really, why should I care? How was it that, in a little more than a week, this small group of inner-city kids had come to mean so much to me? A week and a half ago I'd been ready to end my life. Now, here I was, sitting in a school bus with a bunch of singing, shouting children.

"Turn here," I said to Brick, pointing to the narrow dirt road that led to the farm.

Joe looked out the front window. I could read his thoughts as his eyes skimmed the rolling hills dotted by hay bales and farm equipment, the changing colors of the trees, the large red barn, and the farmhouse. My home was more than he'd imagined it to be. He looked at me, smiled as though he were embarrassed at being caught taking it all in.

He turned in his seat. "How's everybody doing back there?"

The kids shouted, dancing in their seats.

"Everybody having fun?"

"Yeah!"

Denise threw back her head and laughed. I looked straight ahead. The lives of everyone on this bus were about to change. I could feel it.

Maybe even mine.

BRICK PARKED THE bus next to the barn. The children filed out in a funny sort of chaotic order. As soon as their feet hit the gravel, they scattered. I stood near the door, with my back pressed against the bus, hands clasped low and in front. Joe stood a few steps away, hands on his hips, breathing deeply, surveying the world around him. Once the kids were all accounted for, Denise walked over to me and said, "This is really special, Sam. Thank you."

I could only nod. My thoughts at that moment had shifted to Billy. At how he would have enjoyed today. The delight of the children. He would have answered their endless questions with patience and knowledge, and he would have made great friends

with Joe and Denise. My childhood would have met my adulthood with grace and laughter.

I felt a tug on my arm, and I looked down to see Keisha's
smiling face beaming up at me. I held out my hand and she took
it. "You ready?" I asked.

She nodded, lips now pressed together in nervous anticipation.
"Come on."

We started toward the barn just as Joe was unloading the
medical apparatus from the bus. "Sam?" he said.

"Yeah?"

"I need somewhere to set this up. A bedroom in the house
maybe?"

He offered no further explanation, and I felt no invitation
for me to inquire. "There's a bedroom on the first floor," I said,
pulling the house keys from my purse and tossing them to him.
"Just off from the living room."

He nodded his thanks before ambling off toward the house.
Once again his hand hovered over his left side and his gait faltered. It took everything I had not to run after him, to help him,
to ask about his medical condition, whatever it may be.

Keisha squeezed my hand, reminding me of my previous
commitment.

"Okay, princess," I said. "Let's go."

As we neared the backside of the barn, I placed my hands
gently over her eyes. "Keep 'em shut, now," I said.

I felt her cheeks rise beneath the palms of my hands. She was
smiling. Cricket clomped to the open barn door, snorting. I felt

Keisha draw back. "It's okay," I whispered, tilting her head up as we stopped to allow Cricket to come the rest of the way.

I removed my hands and squatted next to Keisha. Her hands instinctively went to Cricket's muzzle and forehead. Wonder filled her eyes.

"Yeah," I said, breathing out. "They're my favorite too."

Her hands continued to explore what she'd only seen in pictures and on television.

"You know they have a special gift, right?"

She looked at me, tilted her head, wanting to know more.

"It's true. Would you like to know what it is?"

Keisha nodded eagerly.

"They keep all your secrets safe. Cricket here knows every one of mine. Happy things. Sad things. And she's never told a soul. You can tell her anything, Keisha, and it'll always be safe."

Keisha looked from me back to the horse. Her dark eyes sparkled with emotion, but I wasn't fully able to read it. Still, if she would venture enough to "talk" to Cricket, perhaps one day she'd talk to me. To Mattie and Macon.

I heard the clearing of a throat. Macon stood at the far corner of the barn, leaning against a door jamb and watching. His eyes locked with mine, the player thanking the one he'd hustled. I knew then just how deep Macon's feelings went for his baby sister, how far down the well of his love ran.

"Hey, Macon," I said.

"I was wondering. What're we gonna do first?"

"Where's Joe?"

Macon shrugged. "Last I saw him, he was heading into your house. Want me to go in there and get him?"

I smiled. "Why don't you do that for me?"

He tore off around the corner of the barn.

"Come on, Keisha," I said. "Wait till you see what I've got planned next."

Chapter Eleven

I STOOD NEXT to Denise, watching the house and waiting for Macon to return with Joe. Around us the children were chanting, "Papa Joe! Papa Joe! Papa Joe!" in an effort to get him to hurry up and join the party.

I kept my eyes on the open French doors, wishing I knew Denise well enough to ask her about Joe. About the apparatus and whether Joe was going to be okay.

Before I could muster up the words to broach the subject, Macon came running out of the doors and onto the porch. Joe walked behind him, slower, but he didn't seem any worse for the wear.

Joe rubbed his hands together and said, "All right, Miss Sam. What's first?"

I tingled with excitement. "How many of you know what a zip line is?"

About a third of the hands went up.

"Well, we have a zip line here. It's fun. It's daring. And I can't help but wonder who will be the first to ride it!"

THE ZIP LINE ran along the length of the creek snaking through our property. As it turned out, the first to ride was Snuffy, and only by luck of the draw.

I'd placed several opened bales of hay for "landing" at the end of the line. Brick decided it best if he stood in front of the hay to catch the kids, just in case one of them landed harder than expected. Sure enough, as Snuffy came soaring down, he crashed full weight into Brick, knocking Brick into the hay. Snuffy landed on top of him.

After that, it became requisite to the fun that Brick stand in front of the hay, take the blow from each kid, and together fall into the hay. By the time the children, Denise, and I had ridden the zip line three times each, the kids had started to complain of hunger.

Brick and I returned to the house where there waited a few coolers full of food I'd prepared the day before. After lunch, the kids stretched out in the grass and napped. The adults were right there with them, including me.

With Detective Miller looking into Anthony Jones's background—and surely he was—and with the cool morning air turning pleasantly warm, I felt as though I could sleep a good two hours before waking. But the children were good for only about a third of that. They were up in no time, running around, chasing the geese and the ducks that had wandered over from one of our ponds. Pretty soon, the geese and the ducks were chasing them, which left Brick, Joe, Denise, and me in fits of laughter.

We returned to the barn so I could introduce the children to Cricket and Penny. I taught the kids about "tacking up" a horse and then put them both on a lead. One by one Brick helped the kids into the horses' saddles, then Denise and I led them around the corral. When everyone—including Joe—had enjoyed a ride, I showed the children what it took to un-tack a horse. "This part is just as important," I said, "even though you're usually tired at the end of a ride."

"Hey, Sam," Macon said, disrupting what I'm sure he found to be quite boring. "There's a cow over here who I'm thinkin' needs milking." He giggled.

"Hey, now," Joe said, placing his hand on Macon's head. "It's impolite to interrupt."

Macon bent his head. "Sorry."

"Tell you what, Macon," I said. "Let's finish up here, and I'll let you milk Miss Maggie Moo."

Minutes later everyone but Macon leaned against the railing that kept Maggie inside her stall. Macon stood inside with the cow.

"Okay, Macon," I said. "What you do is, first drag the stool over to Maggie."

Macon obediently did as instructed.

"Now, what you want to do is—"

Macon held up a hand to stop me. "Naw. I got this. Seen this a million times on TV."

"Well . . . all right then . . ."

"See, you just grab one of these thingies and pull."

Just as I expected, when Macon grabbed one of Maggie's udders and pulled, milk sprayed him in the face.

"Aww, man!"

The children laughed heartily as Macon wiped his face with his sleeve.

"Sorry about that," I said. "But I tell you what—I'll finish milking Maggie later on. If you want, there's a bag of lollipops stashed in that cabinet over there. You can go get them and pass them out to everyone."

A relieved Macon stood. I inched into the stall, making certain everyone had a clear view of Macon as he opened the cabinet doors.

Whoosh! Three hens I'd stashed there earlier flew out, landing Macon on his rear end. Unlike Billy, he was not amused. But everyone else was. The laughter was infectious.

Macon turned to glare at me, and I gave him my best "I just got you back so good" look.

"Whoops. Sorry about that," I said, stepping between his sprawled legs. I reached inside and brought out the bag of lollipops. "Who wants to hand these out?" I asked.

One of the older girls came forward, taking the bag from me, but not before I pulled out a cherry one. I knelt beside Macon, who'd sat halfway up and rested on his elbows. Chicken feathers stuck to his hair. "Here you go, Macon."

He grimaced, but he took it anyway. "Thanks."

"Hey," I said low enough that no one else could hear. "Bringing everyone out to the farm was a wonderful idea. I'm so glad you thought of it."

I stood before he could counter and returned to where Joe was leaning against Maggie's stall railing. His forehead was beaded with sweat. "Joe? Are you—are you okay?"

He grimaced. Swallowed. "No worries." He blew pent-up air from his lungs. "What's next?"

I didn't like this, but it was obvious he wasn't going to answer me truthfully. "There's a waterfall alongside one of the ponds. I was thinking we could carry some construction paper down there. Show the kids how to make paper boats?"

"Sounds good."

"There are also a few paddleboats. How does that sound?"

He avoided looking at me. "Very good."

"Joe?"

But he stepped away, clapping his hands. "Hey, kids! How'd you like to see a waterfall?"

WE LOADED THE kids onto a hay-filled trailer hitched to a tractor. I handed the keys to Brick, gave him general directions, and then joined the others on the trailer. When we'd gone as far as we could, Brick stopped the tractor. I leapt down, calling for the children to follow me. We hiked through a field of calf-high grass for ten minutes before the sound of the waterfall reached our ears.

"Listen," I said. "That sound you hear is a waterfall. Anyone here ever see a waterfall?"

Fifteen heads shook no.

"A waterfall is what happens when water from a river pours over the rocks like a giant shower in a bathtub. And it's just around that bend," I said, pointing. "Who wants to see?"

"We do! We do!"

"Then *go*," I said, clapping my hands.

They took off running. Joe, Brick, Denise, and I brought up the rear at a slower pace. None of us said anything. None of us had to. Everything was perfect, just the way it was. And I . . . I couldn't believe how tired I was. Or how happy.

Later, when the paper boats had set sail and all the little hands had dipped into the cascade of water, Joe and I sat shoulder to shoulder on one of the rocky benches nature had carved next to the waterfall. Brick and Macon were standing near the waterfall, cupping water into their hands and splashing each other. Keisha sat quietly on the bank of the pond, drawing in her sketchbook. Out in the water, Denise and Chloe circled around in a paddle-boat. I looked casually over to Joe, to find him intently watching the two of them.

I smiled knowingly.

Joe turned, catching me. "What?"

"You don't see it, do you?"

"What? See what?"

I turned my face toward the water, toward Denise and Chloe, then back to Joe.

Sheepishly he ducked his head. I bopped him with my shoulder, and he laughed. "Aww, come on."

"Uh-huh."

"Come on." But he laughed.

"She's special," I said.

"I know that's right."

And then, for the first time in hours, I felt lonely. Missing Billy so much my heart ached. "Don't miss out on special, Joe," I told him.

His eyes searched mine. As much as I didn't know what was going on with him, what had taken him to the Commons, or why he was sick . . . I realized, Joe didn't know about me, either. About my life. About my life with Billy. And about what I'd lost when he died.

WITH DARK SETTLING in and around the farm, we ushered the children into the house so they could wash their hands and faces before heading back out to the barn. While Brick and Denise prepared the planned cookout featuring beanie-weenies and a fresh green salad (whether the kids liked it or not), I stayed inside to make pans of hot cornbread.

Joe was the last to come out of the downstairs bath.

"Hey, Joe," I called from the kitchen.

He turned to look at me but didn't walk over. Maybe he was afraid I'd ask about the medical equipment he'd set up in the downstairs bedroom. Or maybe he was just anxious to help Denise and Brick. To be with his kids. Either way, he stayed put on the far side of the sofa, hands resting easily on his hips.

I said, "I just wanted to tell you that yesterday I hung some Chinese paper lanterns in a section of the barn. All you need to do is plug them in. And there's a big washtub full of drinks near the back of the barn. There's a chest-style freezer with bags of ice. Just add the ice to the bucket."

"Gotcha." He nodded once.

"There's some old cable spools out there too. I put a stack of checkered tablecloths on top of one of them. Get Brick to help you set them up. They'll be perfect for the kids to eat off of."

"Yes, ma'am."

I smiled as the oven dinged, telling me it had preheated and was ready. When I opened the door, I felt the heat hit my face.

"Sam?"

I slid the pans in and closed the door before looking back at Joe.

"I just wanted to say it again."

"What?"

"Thank you."

I was momentarily at a loss for words. In many ways I should be thanking him. "It's nothing."

He shook his head. "It's not nothing. It may seem like a little thing to you . . ." His eyes wandered to the yard outside between the house and the barn where the children ran in circles, shouting and singing. "But to them, it's everything."

"Well then," I said, "we'll have to do it again."

He nodded once more before walking out the French doors, leaving me alone with my task and my thoughts. We could have done this, I thought. Billy and me. If we'd known. So many opportunities wasted. Not because we didn't care. Billy would have cared to the nth degree. But more because we hadn't known.

Well, now I did know. And purpose had come back to me in a strange new way. Something I'd never counted on, from someone I'd nearly forgotten. Life sure was strange sometimes. And—when we allowed it to be—full of surprises.

While the cornbread baked, I went upstairs to wash my face and brush my teeth and hair. My bed begged me to come lay across it, but I didn't dare. I would certainly fall fast asleep, even with all the noise from outside.

I had left my cell phone on the bedside table. I checked it to see if Detective Miller had called me back, but there were no missed calls. No messages. I pulled a heavier jacket from my closet and tucked the phone inside the pocket.

I went back downstairs and waited at the kitchen table for the cornbread to be done. Its delightful aroma filled the room. As the timer neared zero, I pulled a large platter from a cabinet and a cutting knife from a drawer and got my oven mitts ready. When the timer beeped, I checked the cornbread. It was perfect. Golden yellow and sweet smelling.

I crossed the now-vacant yard to the barn, balancing the two trays, the platter, and a cutting knife in both hands. I could see Denise and Brick taking plates of food to the makeshift tables where most of the children had gathered. But across the way, I could also see Macon, Snuffy, and another young man named Darren standing at Billy's record player. Darren had put on Billy's hard hat, and Macon was drawing the needle toward the last record Billy had played. The one I'd never taken off the turntable. As soon as the music started, the boys covered their ears.

I couldn't make it to them fast enough. "Hey, guys . . ." I tried to keep my voice calm. After all, they had no idea what they were touching. How valuable it was to me. Nor did they know about the remarkable man who'd once stood under the hard hat.

"I would rather you wouldn't . . ." I placed the cornbread on a nearby cable spool, one that hadn't been dragged to the center of the room and covered with blue-and-white-checkered plastic. ". . . play over here, okay?" I pulled the hard hat from Darren's head. "I'm sorry."

I removed the needle from the old record and flipped the switch to OFF.

"Miss Sam's right, y'all."

I returned the hard hat to where I kept it before turning to see Joe standing over the record player. He picked up the album cover laying on the table next to it and ran his hand over it, removing the dust. "This is real special stuff right here."

"This stuff?" Macon asked. "I ain't never heard music like this, man."

"It's called country music. Honky-tonk. And you just may find it interesting to know, Mr. Macon, that this girl's music helped save my life once."

"Say what?"

"Yes, sir. Back when I was in prison."

Prison? When had Joe been in prison? I looked at the boys, but none of their faces registered surprise. The fact of Joe's having been incarcerated—when and for what, notwithstanding—was not news to them.

"Oh, I gotta hear about this," Macon said, shifting his weight from one foot to the other.

"Y'all don't wanna hear none-a that."

The boys looked at each other, eyes wide with want. But before they could say anything, I spoke.

"Oh, yes we would."

Joe looked me in the eye. He reached over to the pan of cornbread, picked up the knife, and sliced a corner piece before bringing it to his mouth and biting into it. "Well," he said around the crumbs, "the first thing you learn in prison is to always, *always* . . ."

Chapter Twelve

". . . MIND YOUR own business.

"It was my first day in. I was nearly twenty-three years old. Ole Samurai Joe was in good shape, and I'd need to be for what I was about to come up against. Not that I understood that at the time.

"It was lunch break. If for no other reason, my men, the food is why you don't *ever* want to go to prison. That day was green beans out of a tin can that must have sucked all the flavor right out of 'em."

The boys giggled, but Joe's expression told them he wasn't kidding.

"Mashed potatoes. And I don't mean your grandma's mashed potatoes. I'm talking about dried flakes they add watered-down milk to so they can *call* it mashed potatoes."

"Eww," Snuffy said.

Bernard sauntered over. "Whatch y'all talking about?"

"About when Papa Joe was in prison," Snuffy answered.

I leaned against the Home Depot locker, Billy's jacket pressed beneath my shoulder. For the briefest of moments, the scent of his old cologne wafted around me.

"And meatloaf," Joe continued. "Or what they *called* meatloaf. I promise you, it wasn't anything you'd want to eat. But they had this cornbread, see. And the cornbread wasn't half bad." Joe raised the slice of my cornbread and took another bite. His eyebrows rose.

"So I got my tray of food and started looking for a place to sit. I noticed this old man—a white dude—sitting all by himself at one of the tables. I was used to sitting with white dudes, not that it made no never-mind to me what color a man was. A place to sit was a place to sit. I walked over and sat down across from the old man. His name was Pauly. I didn't know that then. I found out later.

"Soon as I sat down, Pauly looked up at me and said, 'Keep on walkin', young buck.' Pauly's hands were shaking, he was so old. He had long, stringy gray hair, and he wore a knit cap to keep his head warm. Pauly looked just like a homeless man who's seen better days. Well, I decided right then and there that I liked Pauly. I said, 'No sir. Think I'm doing just fine right here.'

"Then I took a bite of the beans. Did I mention how nasty they were?"

The boys nodded. I crossed my arms over my middle, wanting him to get on with his story. Wanting to know why he was in prison, much less sampling the food there.

"Pauly said, 'Got rules here. That's why you gotta move it. Now scat 'fore I get angry.' But I didn't flinch. Didn't move a muscle except to eat. Pauly sighed—he realized I wasn't going anywhere. That I was born stubborn, like my grandma used to say. So he said, 'You gonna eat that cornbread?' That was Pauly's way of saying we were okay. And as good of friends as we could be, given where we were. I wanted the cornbread, oh yes, I did. It was the only decent thing on the plate. But I wanted Pauly to have it more. So I handed him my cornbread. Just then I felt this powerful presence come up behind me, and I heard a booming voice say, 'Take a walk.'

"I glanced over my shoulder. Now, this brother was huge. 'You talkin' to me, tubby?' Pauly asked him, and he kinda smiled. But then his smile disappeared and his eyes moved down a little. I turned again. 'Tubby' had a shank in his hand, half hidden under the front of his shirt.

"I know you all know what a shank is. And Pauly knew too. He picked up his tray and slid out from his seat. 'Yes sir,' he said. 'I was just leaving.' Pauly didn't even turn around and look at me when he walked away.

"The big dude—his name was Big Mac—now this was one mean man. Built like a defensive lineman. He walked over and sat down where Pauly had been. Looked me dead in the eye. His entourage—his bunch of thug backups—stood around him, peering down on me like I was a mosquito that needed to be swatted.

"Big Mac pointed to something that had caught his attention, something behind me. He said, 'See that?' And I turned to look . . ."

"What was it, Papa Joe?" Bernard asked.

"Y'all know who Dr. Martin Luther King Junior was, right?"

Everyone nodded. I looked over to Denise, who was taking care of the other children with Brick. She glanced over and smiled.

"Dr. King was killed by a man named James Earl Ray. What Big Mac was pointing to was an old, shackled prisoner being brought into the cafeteria by two armed guards. 'That old man there,' Big Mac said. 'That's James Earl Ray. Man who shot Dr. King. Every time I see his face, it reminds me there *cain't* be no peace between us and them, you got me? Dr. King was fool enough to dream it. And look where it got him.' Big Mac shook his head. He stood up. And then he leaned over, putting both of his giant hands flat down on the table. 'You new here,' he said to me, 'so I'm gonna let you off with a warnin'. Stay with yo' own kind, sheep. Or Big Mac's gonna have to put his hands on somebody.'"

"What did *you* say?" Macon asked, his voice quieter, more subdued than I'd ever heard it.

I knew how he felt. I was barely breathing at this point.

"I didn't say nothin', Macon," Joe continued. "There's a time to talk and a time to keep your mouth shut. That was the time to keep my mouth shut."

"Was there ever a time to talk?" Darren asked.

"Sort of."

"What does *that* mean?" Macon asked, crossing his arms, leaning back against the table with the record player on top. I started to reach out, to protect it from getting knocked over, but I didn't want to interrupt Joe.

"It means, there was a time to *sing*. See, me and another prisoner—a brother named Grady—were in our cell block atrium. All the other prisoners were in their cells, blacks on one side, whites on the other, except Grady and me. Know why?"

"'Cause you were cool?" Macon asked.

I rolled my eyes.

"No. Because Grady and I had to mop the whole cell block. Upstairs. Downstairs. The guards were playing this hillbilly music . . ." He pointed to the album cover still in his hand. ". . . on a record player just like this one. Sitting on a table. Big speakers on either side. Grady *hated* this kind of music. And, I guess, he'd gotten a little tired of it. A little cranky. He said, 'I can't listen to this trash no more! Can't a brotha get some r-e-s-p-e-c-t?'

"I looked up to where the guard tower was. It had a solid glass wall so they could watch our every move. Those two guards were snickering at Grady, and I could smell trouble. 'Shut up, man,' I told him. 'Just mop.'

"About that time one of the white prisoners—guy named Wesley—pressed his face up against the bars of his cell."

Joe's face changed as he spoke. His words became whisper soft. It pained him to say these things. I understood. There were things about Billy, about his death, that I couldn't tell another living soul. Somehow Joe had managed to not only come to this point, but he was effectively sharing it with children. I couldn't imagine what he was about to say, but whatever it was, it carried more than just a bad memory; it carried a bad feeling.

"Wesley's head was shaved, and he had a big tattoo of a spider over his right ear. He liked chewing tobacco. That day he had a mouthful of chaw in his gums. He spit it between the bars, and it landed right where Grady had just mopped. 'Hey,' he said to Grady. 'You missed a spot.' Well, that did it for Grady. He dropped his mop and headed straight for that record player.

"'Don't do it, man,' I told him.

"But Grady picked the needle up off the record player, anyway, scratching the record as he did.

"He shouted, 'Take this, crackers!'"

Joe shook his head. He took in a deep breath through his nostrils, then blew it out his mouth. "That whole cell block went quiet, until one of the white prisoners started shaking the bars of his cell. Then another. And another. All of a sudden I hear the buzzer sound. Cell doors start opening. Only the white prisoners' cells, though. I looked back up to the tower. The guards had set to amusing themselves, and Grady and I were going to be the entertainment."

I swallowed hard, wondering where this story was leading.

"Big scary tattooed white men. Shuffling toward Grady and me. The brothers were rattling the doors to their cells now. Shouting to get out. To protect their fellow brothers. Grady reached down and picked up his mop." Joe chuckled. "Like that was gonna help. Some weapon a mop handle was against these guys. No more use against them than a rattlesnake. We started backing up.

"I said to Grady, 'If we live through this, remind me to kill you later.' Then I took a deep breath and stepped toward the record player, real casual-like. Held up my hand like this . . ." Joe demonstrated a slight wave of the hand, as though he were saying, "Give me a minute here."

"I put the needle back on the record. Put it on the second song and started singing along. *Darlin', I'm breakin' outta here today* . . ." Joe laughed. "Those white dudes didn't know what to think. How was it this brother knew the lyrics to a country song? But what they didn't know was about me and Miss Sam, you see. Country's all Sam and my other friends from childhood would listen to. Must-a heard that tune a thousand times.

"Next thing I know, I hear another man singing, and he's doing it even louder than me. It was Pauly." Joe smiled. "He walked up next to me, and we sang a duet for our audience. Pauly got a little excited, though. He slammed his hand down on the table, the needle jumped off the record, and the whole thing shut down.

"Now Pauly and me are standing there—one white dude and one black brother—breathin' heavy and waitin' for someone to make the next move."

I spoke without thinking, "Who did?" I blinked several times, my own voice bringing me back to the barn. I'd been so totally immersed in Joe's story, I hadn't noticed that all the children had joined us and were sitting at Joe's feet, listening. Denise and Brick stood close by, both nodding their approval.

Joe smiled at me. "Wesley. He steps up to me, sizes me up one side and down the other, and says, 'Know any Hank Williams?'

"'Know 'em all,' I told him. 'Which one we doin'?'"

"Wesley was impressed. White dudes are laughing now. They're happy, and Grady is relieved to know he's going to live to see another day. Then the guards shouted, 'Okay, ladies. That's enough. Back to your cells.' They'd had their entertainment, and the show was over."

I turned to look inside the locker, to flip through some of Billy's old LPs, knowing somehow that it was time. Time to do what I hadn't been able to do for three years: put another record on the turntable.

I wrapped my fingers around the top of one of the albums, looked over at Joe, and found him looking straight at me.

"Maybe Miss Sam saved my life twice, come to think of it."

I rolled my eyes while the children laughed.

I pulled the album from the stack and handed it slowly toward him. Doing this—allowing him to take the record—meant he'd want to play it as soon as he saw whose it was. He'd take the last record Billy had played and replace it with this one. I'd be letting go. Right here, with the children around me. And Denise and Brick and Joe. They'd have no idea, of course. No clue what it meant to me, doing this. What courage it would take.

"No way," Joe said, taking the album from my hand.

As I expected, he slid the album from the cover and the sleeve, then carefully replaced the one from Billy's last evening in the barn.

I took in a sharp breath. Closed my eyes. Like removing a Band-Aid, in one quick moment, it was over.

"We gonna blow it up with this one here," Joe said.

The children laughed loudly. I opened my eyes. Joe's fingers lightly dropped the needle to the vinyl. He turned up the volume, filling the barn with music.

"Yeah! C'mon, y'all!" Joe started wiggling around, popping himself on his hip like a bronco riding a wild horse. In no time the kids, Brick, and Denise were up and joining in, doing the same. I'd never seen anything quite like it. Fifteen black children, two black adults, and one white bus driver doing what might could have passed for the Virginia Reel. I brought my hands up to my lips. My fingertips rested on a smile I'd not realized had formed.

I started laughing then. Slowly at first, then with everything I had in me. Denise and Joe do-si-doed, surrounded by the children. Even quiet Keisha was jumping up and down, joining in the play without reservation.

Just then I heard my cell phone ring from the recesses of my coat pocket. I pulled it out and checked the caller ID.

Detective Miller.

He was calling me back.

Chapter Thirteen

I STEPPED OUTSIDE of the barn as quickly as I could, flipping my phone open as soon as I was away from the noise.

"Detective Miller?"

"Mrs. Crawford, I got your message concerning Anthony Jones . . ."

I took in a deep breath. This was it. I could tell by the tone of his voice he had something important to tell me. "So you ran the name?"

"Didn't have to. Your boy was one of our original suspects."

Hope seeped out of my lungs like a slow leak from a child's balloon.

"But he had an alibi. He was with his cousin that night."

I pressed my hand up to my forehead, pushing hair away from my face. I looked down at my boots, feeling dizzy. I'd been so sure. The clippings . . .

"But I'm telling you, I saw—"

"I don't really care what you saw, Mrs. Crawford. I care about evidence. I can't make an arrest in a homicide case based on your gut feelings." I heard him sigh deeply. "Look, just stay out of the Commons, you hear? Nothing good ever comes outta that place . . ."

I stood straight, looked over my shoulder at the children, still dancing. To Keisha, who twirled under Joe's guiding hand.

"And nothing good ever will," Detective Miller finished. "Look, whatever it is you're doing down there, you need to stop. And don't call me about this again, you hear me? You're on your own."

I opened my mouth to tell him I *was* doing something good, that he didn't know what I knew. To tell him about the box in Anthony Jones's drawer. The box I *knew* held the truth. But before I could say another word, Detective Miller disconnected the call.

Dismissed. Just like that.

And just like that, Billy's murderer would go free.

I decided that Detective Miller was a cruel man. He didn't care. Didn't care about Billy. About me. About finding the truth.

I slowly turned and walked back into the barn where the party continued. Scraped-clean paper plates littered the makeshift tables, half-empty drink bottles abandoned around them. My guests continued to laugh and smile and dance while I now found it difficult to breathe.

I took the stairs up to the loft. When I had reached the top, I peered over the railing. Beneath the glow of the Chinese lanterns, my new friends kicked up the hay, unaware of what I was feeling in this moment. So much joy below, so much distress above.

I turned toward the corkboard and the table with my paints, pencils, and artwork, feeling every bit as hopeless as I had the night I'd met Keisha and Macon. The night I'd seen Joe again for the first time in ages.

Taking deliberate steps forward, I focused on my drawing of the man in the red hoodie. This drawing was of Anthony Jones. I knew it. I slowly removed the tack holding it in place and examined the sketch. I now had a face I could add to the phantom gangster. With a little effort, I could have it filled out.

"So this is where you hide out." Joe's voice came from behind me.

I whirled around, hiding the sketch behind my back.

Joe stood at the top of the stairs, watching me. "What is all this?"

I dropped the sketch to the table and, turning, covered it with another drawing, something I had worked on for *Firebird*.

"Wow. What is all this?" Joe asked again, his footsteps drawing closer as the music continued to play beneath us. I scooped up about twelve paintbrushes scattered near my fingertips and returned them to one of the Mason jars where they belonged.

Joe now stood next to me, his fingers lightly touching some of my awards and trophies.

"This is my life," I said.

He looked up at the shelf where I kept first-print copies of all my books. "Are all these yours?"

"Yeah." I felt nervous. Uncomfortable. No one but my husband and parents had been up here before now.

"Hey," he said, pointing to a drawing like the one of the little oriole I'd drawn the night of the campout with Billy. "There's that little bird you were always drawing. You write that book?"

My eyes fell to the sketch pad set aside for *Firebird*. Joe followed my gaze, picked it up, and thumbed through it. There was nothing but blank pages.

He gave me a questioning look.

"No, I gave up on it," I said, working furiously at looking busy, moving pieces of paper around on my desk.

"Why?"

It's about a little bird who finds out that God even cares for the sparrows. Then he's happy.

"Because I don't believe it anymore."

Joe inched closer. With hands shaking, I pulled the padded stool out from under the desk and sat on it, keeping my face turned away from his. One look at him, I knew, and my resolve would crumble. If that happened, I wasn't sure I could regain my composure. The children were still downstairs, still laughing, still playing. If the dam burst, I was certain they'd hear the anguish I felt in my heart. I couldn't let that happen. These children, they didn't deserve to hear that.

"Hey now," Joe whispered.

Keeping my head down, I cast my eyes his way. He now leaned back against the desk, his legs crossed at the ankles. I kept my focus on his boots, even more so on the shoelaces.

Anything to keep from crying.

"Hey," he said again. "What happened, Sam? Where's that hopeful little girl I knew?"

I opened my mouth to answer. To say something positive. But the words wouldn't come. Couldn't make it past the knot that had formed in my throat.

Tears welled up in my eyes and spilled down my cheeks.

My chest hurt. If I didn't let it go, I was afraid of what might happen next. "She died," I said, pressing my face into my hands, the tears now coming without apology.

Joe stepped around me, wrapped his arms around my shoulders, and pulled my face to his chest. I inhaled deeply. He smelled of sunshine and hay. Love and friendship. The tenderness of his embrace was not lost on me. I needed this. I needed someone I could trust to hold me. To tell me it would be okay. That life would be okay. That I would be happy again, and one day I'd look forward to the rising of the sun.

The next moment I felt silly and ashamed. How was it, I wondered, that Joe—with everything he'd obviously been through—had found such purpose and I could not?

Joe tucked my head under his chin. "Do you want to talk about it?" he whispered.

I shook my head. "Not right now. I can't . . . not right now."

I felt him nod. "I'm here when you need me."

This only made me cry harder.

Joe didn't say another word. He simply stood there with his arms around me, hands awkwardly rubbing between my shoulder blades in small circles, waiting for the tears to subside and my anguish to ease. When I was finally done, I looked up at him through wet lashes.

"I guess I'm a mess."

He smiled. "I guess you are."

Which made me chuckle.

"Sounds like things are winding down, down there," he said. "I'm gonna help Denise and Brick get the kids turned in for the night."

"Okay." I smiled up at him. "Thank you, Joe."

"Any time."

I watched him shuffle across the loft and then step slowly down the stairs. Just before his head disappeared beneath the floorboards, he looked over at me. Offered a single nod. I smiled again in return.

After a few minutes, I heard Denise call, "All right, everyone. Time to pick up, clean up, and head on back to the house."

Mumbles of disappointment rose on the rafters. I walked over to the stairs, sat on the top step, and leaned my head against a rail, watching the activity below. Joe leaned against the barn door, oblivious to me. Denise walked backward toward him, her eyes still on the children. But when she reached Joe, she turned, stood shoulder to shoulder with him, and smiled.

He looked at her intently until a pained look crossed his face.

"Hey, old man," she said. "You do your dialysis today?"

I sucked in a breath as Joe pressed his lips together and shook his head. "No, ma'am."

Denise crossed her arms.

"But I will. I promise."

Dialysis. That was the machine I'd seen in his bedroom in Nashville. The one he'd brought to the farm. That meant something was wrong with Joe's kidneys.

Denise clasped her hands together and brought them to her chest, as though she were in prayer. "Were you upstairs talking to Sam?"

He nodded, keeping his eyes on hers. For a moment I watched them do what Billy and I had once been able to do—speak without words.

"Everything all right?"

Joe answered with a shrug.

"Tell you what. Brick and I can get the kids to bed. Why don't you spend as much time as you need with her?"

Joe gave her a questioning look.

"She needs you, Joe."

I drew my knees close to my chest and wrapped my arms around them. Denise had to be the most giving person I'd ever had the privilege of knowing. And that included Billy.

"But you'll owe me one," she continued, smiling.

Joe appeared confused. "Owe you? Owe you what?"

Her smile grew wider, which made me smile too. If Joe hadn't known about Denise's feelings for him before now, surely he couldn't deny them after this. "I'm sure you'll think of something."

The light from the Chinese lanterns was shut off about five seconds before the children and Brick, who carried one sleeping child in his arms, started filling the spaces around Joe and Denise, Keisha lagging behind. Only the light from outside over the barn door illuminated them. I turned my head to look to where the party had just concluded. Toward the back, Cricket had stuck her head out of her stall and was watching the processional.

"Come on, little buckaroos," Denise said.

Joe kicked his heel against the hay-strewn packed dirt. "I'll walk you halfway."

I sat and waited, closing my tired eyes, knowing Joe would be back any minute. When I heard the sound of feet, I opened my eyes again to see Keisha walking ever so slowly into the barn. She walked all the way to the back, to where bales of hay were stacked high, and her backpack lay propped against the base of them. With one swoop, she picked it up and swung it over her shoulder, and then took two steps toward the barn door.

But then she stopped and, head cocked, looked over at Cricket.

I placed my hand over my mouth and watched as she took cautious steps toward the horse. When she was near enough, Cricket leaned down, allowing Keisha to place her head against the horse's long nose. Cricket snorted as though giving permission. Then, ever so gently, Keisha raised a hand to Cricket's ear, bent it forward, and whispered into it.

Moments later Keisha walked out the door, toward the farmhouse.

Tears sprang to my eyes.

Keisha had spoken. She'd shared her secrets with Cricket.

WHEN JOE REAPPEARED, I was standing at the barn door, struggling with whether or not to tell him what I'd seen.

"Wanna take a walk?" he asked.

"Part of the creek runs behind the barn over here," I said. "Just past the hay bales."

"Show me."

We walked side by side, neither of us saying anything until we reached the creek. By then I'd decided to let Keisha's secret remain between her and Cricket. I picked up a few pebbles and flung them, and they skipped across the water in the moonlight. Joe eased himself down, stretched out his legs, and invited me to do the same.

Closing my eyes, I took in the evening sounds around us. The movement of water over the river rocks. The crickets singing as a breeze whispered gently through the pine needles and the leaves of the oaks and poplars.

"I'm listening when you're ready," Joe said.

I ran my palms down the top front of my jeans. "My husband's name was Billy. We met when I was in college. He was the cousin of my roommate and . . . I'd been invited to her house for the weekend." I looked out over the water. "She lived not . . . not too far from here."

Joe nodded as he rested his hands behind him in a patch of grass and pine needles.

"Anyway, Billy came over to Julie's house that weekend and . . . one look at him, and I was so madly in love, Joe, I could hardly see a step in front of me."

Joe chuckled.

"I know that sounds silly."

"Naw. Not from a romantic like you, it doesn't."

"He was five years older than me. Life had kept him from going to college. He'd already been working for the power company for years when we met.

"His mama and daddy owned this farm, and he ran that too. They'd moved down to Florida after his daddy said he couldn't take any more of the winter weather."

"I understand that."

"I think they just wanted to live near Mickey Mouse."

Joe smiled.

"Billy and I got married a year after we met. I finished school and took an internship at a publishing house in Nashville. Wrote my first book. And then my second. Neither got published." I laughed lightly. "At the time, I only had three fans. One I was married to, and the other two had brought me into this world. But my third book caught the attention of one of the editors. I got myself an agent, and the next thing I knew, I had a career writing children's books."

"An award-winning career."

I nodded.

"I always knew you had it in you."

I glanced upward to the slivers of sky I could see between the tree branches. To the stars and the moon. "You thought my stories were silly."

"Aww, I just said that. Deep down," he said, pointing to his chest, "I always knew."

"Well, thank you for keeping me in the dark all those years."

We shared a smiled. Joe took in a deep breath and exhaled. "So where is Billy now?"

"Three years ago, there was a storm, and Billy got an emergency call to go down near Murphy's Liquor Store."

"Down in the projects?"

"Yes."

"Okay . . ."

"While he was there . . . someone shot and killed him."

Joe grimaced. "Oh, Sam . . ."

Tears filled my eyes. "They never caught the guy who did it. And after a phone call I got tonight from the detective on the case, I don't think they ever will."

"Why? What happened?"

"I thought that I—that maybe I'd seen something in the Commons that might be a clue to his murder. But Detective Miller told me I was mistaken."

"What did you see?"

"It doesn't matter."

Joe chewed on the inside of his lip, and then he smiled, changing the subject. "All right, then. Tell me something else about Billy."

I pulled my legs up so that I was sitting with them crossed. "He gave away two-dollar bills," I said.

"Oh yeah? Why's that?"

"It was his symbol of love. Millions in print, more than enough to go around. But people hoard them, he said. So he came up with the idea to give them away to total strangers. A simple act of kindness." I blinked back tears, too tired to shed any more that night. "When I got his wallet back from the detectives, there were only two things missing. He carried with him a picture of the little oriole, like the one hanging up in the loft. It was gone. And there were no two-dollar bills. Either he'd given them all away, or someone had taken them."

Taken away all the love Billy had to give, in more ways than one.

"He sounds like a wonderful man," Joe said.

"He was."

Joe grinned. "So then why'd he pick you?"

I swatted at him, and he chuckled.

But then I grew serious. "Joe, you asked me up there what had happened to the little girl you knew. Now you know. But what about you? You've changed a lot too."

"Yeah." He shifted his weight, winced. "Yeah, I have."

"Joe? What's going on?"

Joe's hand hovered over his left side as I'd seen it do several times before. "Well," he finally said, "I guess I owe you that."

Chapter Fourteen

"BOTH MY KIDNEYS shut down a few years back," he said. "Permanent disability. Basically what that means is, I went from prison to the projects."

"Did you have—develop—diabetes or something?"

He shook his head. "Luck of the draw. I've got what they call FSGS, which is an easy way to say Focal Segmental Glomerulosclerosis." He winked. "Say that three times fast."

I smiled back. "Say it? I've never even heard of it."

"Few have. It's rare and it's . . . well, it's just one of those things that happens."

Just one of those things.

I wasn't sure if I was ready or willing to fall into that conversation, so I opted for more information on his other shocking revelation. "How long were you in there? In prison?"

"Got eight years."

"For?"

"Stealing two hundred bucks."

I couldn't believe what I was hearing. Joe? Stealing? In spite of his family's poverty, he'd excelled at everything he'd done. Music. Academics. And of course, martial arts. It wasn't like the boy I knew to stoop to stealing, much less such a little amount of money. "What happened? Exactly?"

"Well, let me back up a little. I graduated top of my class in high school, did you know that?"

I shook my head. Joe and I had ended up in different schools after elementary school. So our friendship had lasted only a handful of years.

"I went to college on a full scholarship in engineering and computer science."

I playfully punched him in the arm. "Look at you . . ."

"Yeah, well. Don't be too impressed. It wasn't always about wanting to do my best. It was more about me wanting to prove I was *worth* something. Always did, I guess. It was important that I show my dad he was wrong for walking out on my mother and me. That I *was* somebody. So I worked hard. Studied hard. And I was at the top of my class in college, just like in high school. I even had a great job lined up with IBM."

He paused long enough, I suppose, for me to take all this in. "And then?"

He sighed. "And then me and some friends got into hacking. Right before graduation, this guy bet me two hundred dollars I couldn't hack into a bank. And you know me and a challenge . . ."

I sure did. One time during May Day Sports Events back at Hazelwood Elementary School, Joe was dared that he couldn't win the sit-up contest. He won, but he could hardly walk for a week. Another time, at lunch, Jimmy said Joe couldn't eat ten hotdogs. Joe took the challenge, ate the hotdogs, and then spent the afternoon in the nurse's office.

"Eight years," I said again, completely dumbfounded by how such a small amount of money could cost a man so much.

As if reading my mind, Joe said, "Sometimes it's the bet you win that ends up costing you the most."

For a fleeting moment I thought about the phone call from Detective Miller. If I were right about Anthony Jones, might it cost me something? Could I be in over my head, trying to do an investigator's job? "You're telling me—"

"Yes, ma'am."

Joe stood, reached out a hand, and helped me to my feet. He placed his hand on the small of my back, turning me back toward the house and barn. But there was no hurry, and our footsteps showed it. We had all night, if need be.

"You never were one to back down from a dare," I said.

"Truth is, that was just an excuse. It was my pride that took me down. Always comes before the fall. Isn't that what the Good Book says?"

"Does it?"

"Something like that." Joe reached over to a shrub and pulled a leaf from it. He rolled it around in between his fingers, then brought it up to his nose, inhaling its fresh scent. "Proverbs 16:18: 'Pride goes before destruction, a haughty spirit before a fall.'"

I grinned at him. "You're just like your grandmother, quoting the Bible."

Joe tossed the leaf into the shrub next to him. "One thing you should know about my story, Sam, is that in the end, it was prison that brought me to God and the greatest revelation of my life."

"How so?"

"Remember me telling the kids back at the barn about the rules of prison?"

"Yeah."

"Well, those rules applied from the cafeteria to the cells and all the way out to the yard."

We'd emerged from the canopy of trees and were standing at the edge of the field where giant bales of hay had been rolled onto their sides. Joe stopped there, the moonlight illuminating his handsome face. "See, I had been sent to Brushy Mountain State Penitentiary, which is maximum security—a place for hardened criminals, which I wasn't. I was only supposed to be there six days. Just enough time to get my work release papers." Joe squinted. "I guess God had other plans.

"During one of those few days, we were all out in the yard. 'Free time' they call it, but that's a misnomer. They got razor wire everywhere. Armed guards in the towers. More guards walking around the grounds with dogs and shotguns." He nodded. "But we were all out there. Segregated, like always. Whites over here, blacks over there. Some of the men were smoking, some playing basketball." He grinned at me. "I was at the exercise equipment, doing pull-ups."

I snickered playfully.

"I'm minding my own business when I hear this ruckus. It's Big Mac and his friends ganging up on old Pauly. See, everyone had gotten past the little fracas over the record player and the singing. Everyone 'cept Big Mac. Now he's yelling at Pauly, gonna make him pay for singing with me. For bringing a few minutes of peace to Brushy.

"I dropped from the bar and started walking toward where they were." Joe licked his upper lip. "Before I could get there, Big Mac had jabbed his fist under Pauly's ribs. I got close enough, I could see blood coming out of the old man's nose."

I sighed. "Oh, Joe . . ."

"Then I heard Pauly say, 'I'm just looking for Joe' to which Big Mac says, 'Yeah, baby? Well, I got somethin' for *you*.'

"I can't get there fast enough, Sam. Big Mac takes out that shank, grabs Pauly by the hand, and slices him." Joe drew an imaginary line across the lifeline of his palm. "Right there."

I balled my hands into fists.

"Pauly cries out. I'm trying to get to him, fast as I can. I hear Big Mac say, 'You've crossed the line. See your white friends over there? They ain't coming 'round here to help you. They know the rules. And you *don't*. So it's just you and me this time.'

"By now I'm close enough to say something and be heard. No shouting necessary. I kept my voice calm but made sure it carried authority, you know what I'm saying?"

I nodded.

"I said, 'You let him go.' Next thing I know, Big Mac's done wrapped his beefy arm around Pauly's neck and got the shank laid up against his throat. Pauly's breath came ragged, he was so scared."

I could barely breathe myself.

"Big Mac said, '*When* I let him go and *how* I let him go is up to you now, sheep.' I could hear the white prisoners backing off and the brothers gatherin' around. 'It's easy,' Big Mac told me. 'Just walk up here and *spit* in this cracka's face.'

"There was so much hate in Big Mac's eyes. Bitterness. Resentment. And nothing but fear in Pauly's. All of a sudden, Big Mac's face changed somehow. Like he was going to say something that made *sense* for a change."

"What did he say?"

"He said, 'Ain't that what they been doing to us for *four hundred years*, my brotha?'"

"I said, 'No.' I'm not sure what I was saying 'no' to, but I said it just the same. One thing I did know, though: I was *not* going to spit in Pauly's face. The man was old. He was feeble. And he was my friend."

"What *did* you do?"

Joe smiled. "Ole Samurai Joe started flexing his muscles, trying to gain some momentum out of the situation. But Big Mac says, 'Boy, you better step up here and spit in this cracka's face.' Pauly looked at me, his eyes all full of sorrow, and he said, 'It's all right, Joe. Just do it.'" Tears shimmered in Joe's eyes.

He shook his head. "But I said, 'No, sir. Not gonna happen.'

"Big Mac started to draw the blade across Pauly's throat. I've never seen so much fear on one man's face in my life.

"'No, please!' Pauly shouted, begging Big Mac not to kill him. All the while, his eyes were pleading with me, *Just do it.*

"'Boy, you spit in this cracka's face, or I'm gonna take a lot more outta him.' Then Big Mac pointed the shank at me. 'Then I take something out of *you*.'

"I've never been so angry in all my life. He wanted to talk about four hundred years? He was sending us *back* four hundred years. And he was using a defenseless old man to do it?

"I said it one more time: 'You best be letting him go.'

"'Or what, sheep?'

"I could tell by the way Pauly's eyes moved that someone was stepping up behind me. Then Big Mac said to whoever it was, 'Get him over here!'"

Joe's face had gone steely. "I took down the one behind me. Then another came at me. I took him down too. Then I heard someone yell, 'Guards comin!'

"Big Mac let go of Pauly. Poor man dropped to his knees and crawled away like a scared dog. Then Big Mac came at me with that shank. It was really me he wanted, anyway. You could see it in his eyes."

Even though logic told me Joe had not been killed in the confrontation, I wasn't sure I liked where this story was heading. "Joe . . ."

"My anger started to boil, Sam. Not just my anger at Big Mac. It was everyone. My father. Every kid who refused to accept me for who I was, not what I looked like. The friend who dared me to hack into that bank." He paused. "Myself. And back to Big Mac again. I mean, here I'd been, put down by most of the white kids for being black, and now I was being put down by a black man for being black."

I thought I understood. A wave of rage had swept over me in the last few minutes, and I didn't even know Pauly or Big Mac.

A thought crossed my mind. Was this how it had been for Billy? Was it because he had been a white man in a predominately black neighborhood? Not robbery, not random violence? But color?

"What did you do?" I asked.

"Big Mac . . . he swung the shank at me. I ducked, jabbed him in the ribs. Heard the breath get knocked out of him. He turned a little to the right, kind of giving in to the pain, so I jabbed him in the lower back. The move made him stumble, and I saw an opportunity. I kicked him behind his knee, buckling him. He went down, and I grabbed his wrist—the one with the shank—and twisted his arm. Hard. I heard him groan, heard the bones crack. I didn't care. Popped his hand so the shank would release." Joe winced again. "Had to pop it twice," he said, showing me the motion, which I was sure had some formal name. Not that it would have mattered if he'd used the actual terminology. I wouldn't have understood any more about the move than I could comprehend that kind of violent behavior.

But what I did recognize was that young "Samori Joe" had, indeed, become the warrior he'd swore he would be when we were children. And that he was now saving the world one child—or one old man—at a time.

Overhead a cloud must have swept across the moon, for we were no longer bathed in its light. A gray shadow had dropped over us, coaxing Joe to continue his story.

"The shank fell to the ground," Joe continued, drawing me back to the prison yard. "Next thing I knew, I had Big Mac flat out, and I was straddled over him. The crowd—black men, white men, didn't make any difference—they was roarin'. I couldn't hear what they were sayin', but I was spurred on by the sound of their voices. I started pounding my fist into Big Mac's face.

Pounding and pounding. One for Pauly. One for me. One for my father, who never cared enough to come see me . . ."

The memory of the little boy lying helpless in the hospital flashed in my mind.

Grandma, how come my dad don't love me?

"Big Mac's face was already swelling. Bloody mess coming out of his mouth and nose. I saw the shank laying not twelve inches from his head. I grabbed it . . ." Joe held his hand up, fist clenched. "I was ready to drive it as deep into that man's chest as it would go. I'd lost all reason. All sanity." Joe shook his head. "Big Mac's eyes were wild. There was more fear in them right then and there than there had been in Pauly's five minutes before. And right then, Sam," he said, looking at me, "I looked down on that man I was about to kill. And in that moment, I saw it so clearly."

"What? What did you see?"

"How far my anger and pride had taken me. How far I had fallen. And how much pain I had caused."

His grandmother. Had she been alive when he was convicted?

"The guards came, and they pulled me off Big Mac. Drug me off to solitary." Joe's expression seemed so far away. "Ever been in solitary, Sam?"

"In some ways, yes."

His brow rose.

"After Billy died. After everyone had gone home and the casseroles ran out and the only place I wanted to be was in the grave, lying next to my husband. I climbed the stairs, got in bed, and hardly came out. After a while, even my mother stopped trying to coax me down." I swallowed. "But I suppose it's different in your case. In mine, I had a choice, I suppose, to walk out any time I wanted. All I had to do was get up and move."

"Yeah. I didn't have that option."

"How long were you in there?"

"Forty days and forty nights. All alone. Guards came three times a day to bring what they called a meal, but other than that, it was just me and God. And, Sam? When God's all you got to talk to, God is *who* you talk to. And you wonder why you didn't talk to Him sooner. Because you see, it was in that darkness, in the loneliest place of all, that I felt the love of a father—*the* Father— for the first time in my life."

A breeze pushed through, pulling the cloud away from the moon. A light was cast across Joe's face. Beads of sweat dotted his forehead and slipped like rivulets down his cheeks and over his jawline.

"I've never been the same since. I feel that love every day I'm with those kids. I look into their eyes and I know: Now *there's* something worth fighting for."

I raised my fingertips to my lips, and they quivered, just as Joe seemed to be. "Samurai Joe. Always the fighter."

But then I realized, Joe wasn't quivering. He was shaking. His left hand pressed under his shirt to his side.

"Sam?" His voice shook. When his hand slipped out from under the hem of the tee, bright red blood lay thick across his fingertips.

He looked from them to me.

"Joe?"

"I think I could use your help . . ."

Chapter Fifteen

I WRAPPED JOE'S arm around my shoulder and carried as much of his weight as I could. The rest was up to him, with what little energy he had left. Being Joe, he didn't give in, and for that I was grateful. I couldn't have carried his entire weight alone.

The scent of hay wafted toward us as we hobbled across the field together. The smell blended with that of burning wood from the living room fireplace. Brick must have lit a fire for the children.

By now, they would be stretched out and asleep in their sleeping bags or on top of the old blankets and quilts their parents and guardians had sent with them. I wondered if Brick or Denise were still awake. I'd told Denise earlier that she was more than welcome to one of the upstairs bedrooms. Brick was going to camp out on the sofa so he could keep watch over the kids and make sure no one got the unction to slip out to the barn during the night.

Perhaps, once I got close enough, I could get his attention.

We'd just made it past the barn when Joe stumbled. "Joe . . ."

He moaned in answer.

I thought of how I'd laid him down in the forest when we were children. How I had run for help. Maybe I should do the same now. "I can go get Brick," I said. "Or Denise . . ."

He stopped long enough to look across the wide expanse of the yard to the house. "No. Just get me to the porch. When you do, get inside as quietly as you can. Go into my room and get the dialysis machine and bring it out to me. I don't want . . . don't want the kids . . ."

"What about Brick?"

"If he's awake, fine. If not . . . we can handle this, Sam. I don't want to take a chance on waking the kids."

I understood. This was far more serious than any of them needed to be a party to. Joe faltered again, and I caught him, carrying his weight with my own. "I've got you, Joe."

It seemed like an eternity, but we made it to the porch. I eased Joe into one of several rockers parked across it. "I'll be right back," I said.

"Quiet now . . ."

I nodded and opened the door with a silent turn of the knob, praying the door didn't creak in protest.

When I stepped into the living room, I found the children lying corner to corner and everywhere in between. Brick's fire continued to blaze in the fireplace, filling the room with warmth. I used its light to guide my feet over and between sleeping children. I glanced to the sofa where Brick snored peacefully, blissfully unaware of Joe's predicament.

I reached the bedroom and rolled the dialysis machine into the hall. Then I picked it up and, as quietly as I could, carried it through the living room. Once the door had closed behind me, I rolled it in haste to where I'd deposited Joe.

Joe's face was bathed in sweat, his eyes wild with pain. He had opened his shirt and pulled his tee up to reveal a port and catheter of some kind. Blood oozed around it, soaking a patch of gauze.

"Good thing I hooked up the fluids earlier," he said, panting.

"Joe, should we take you to the hospital? Or call an ambulance?"

"No," he groaned, and I could feel panic rising.

"Look at me," he said.

I did.

"You can do this, Sam."

I nodded and began instinctively unraveling cords and tubes as though I'd been doing it all my life.

"Plug it in, Sam," he said, the words coming between breaths.

I reached for the electrical cord. An outside outlet was only a few feet away, near the door. I did as Joe instructed.

"Come on," Joe said, his breathing increasingly ragged. He had one of the tubes, but his hand shook too violently to get it to the catheter.

I took the tubes from him. "Here," I said. "Give them to me."

"Hit the switch in the back." Joe's head lolled against the back of the chair.

I did as he said, and the apparatus sprang to life, emitting a series of beeps and tones.

"Take that tube," he said, looking at the machine.

"Which one? There are so many."

"That one." He pointed.

I retrieved the tube he'd indicated.

His hand trembled over the bloody gauze and catheter. "Hook it up," he said. "Ughhhh . . . right in here."

Oh, dear God in heaven, was I adding pain to his agony? "Am I doing this right? Joe?"

"You're fine . . . you're fine."

"Okay . . ."

"You're doing good."

"Okay."

I followed his eyes to where they gazed upon the machine. It blinked words and numbers in codes I didn't understand. "Unclamp that . . ."

"Okay."

". . . and hit the red button."

I did. The beeping from the machine stopped, followed by a gentle clicking and then a *whoosh . . . whoosh . . . whoosh.* Joe groaned a final time—only this time, in relief. I leaned toward him. His left arm—the one closest to the machine—fell across mine, and his hand gently dropped on my shoulder. I felt his fingers wrap themselves into my hair. He coughed a few times before taking in a deep breath and letting it go. Finally he looked up at me. Though his smile was weak, his words held the humor I'd always come to expect from Joe.

"I guess that makes three times, huh?"

I laid my hand on his shoulder and brought the back of my fingers to rest upon his cheek where a five o'clock shadow had grown thick. "Yeah," I said in a whisper. "I guess so."

A SHORT WHILE later, as the dialysis machine hummed beside Joe, another cloud passed across the moon. Joe and I sat side by side on the front porch. I'd gotten a blanket for him and laid it over his lap for warmth. But when the chill in the night air grew heavier, I walked over to the barn where I kept the fire pit and brought it back.

"You're like a pioneer girl," Joe said, watching me throw in firewood and kindling.

I looked up at him and smiled. "Billy and I used to enjoy camping. He was always in charge of the fire-making, but I know how if I need to."

"A regular Laura Ingalls Wilder." He smiled.

I chuckled. "Maybe not that much of a pioneer, though I wouldn't mind being compared to her as an author."

"There ya go . . ."

With the fire blazing, I sat down again next to Joe. "You doing okay?" I asked.

He nodded then sighed as though all was right with his world. "I'll be fine, Dr. Sam."

I crossed my legs and tucked my folded hands between them. "I would if I had to, but I'd rather not have to do that again." I smiled, then grew serious, "Joe? How long can you keep this up?"

"Until the doctor says my kidneys are at the end of their rope and I have to have a transplant."

"Is it dangerous to wait?"

"Could be. But it's the only choice they're givin' me right now."

I heard one of the French doors squeak open. Both Joe and I turned. I fully expected to see Denise, but instead, it was a sleepy-eyed Keisha wrapped in a blanket.

"She's sleepwalking," Joe said. "Mattie says she does it all the time."

I reached my arms toward her. "Come here, baby."

She climbed into my lap, and I drew her close to my chest. I laid her head on my shoulder and watched her heavy eyes close as she drifted back to sleep. In that moment I regretted never having children with Billy. We'd always planned on it, and we did nothing to prevent it. It just never seemed to happen. We'd never fretted over it, never got concerned enough to seek medical advice. We thought we had time.

Keisha's feet wiggled beneath the blanket until ten precious little toes were exposed to the night air. Tenderly, like a father, Joe took the edge of his blanket and placed it over her bare feet. "This child," he said, "is an angel."

I looked down at her, unable to argue the point. If there were angels on earth, then I was surely holding one in my arms now. "She's sound asleep," I said to Joe, then I smiled. "Just listen to her breathing."

"No more peaceful sound on earth."

"Joe," I said, rocking back and forth, back and forth. "What happened to their father and mother?"

Joe's expression turned painful, but this time I knew it wasn't because of the discomfort in his body. This time, it was for Keisha and Macon. "Their mama got caught up with the wrong crowd. One night, when Macon was over at a friend's, a man broke into the house. Keisha ran into the kitchen and hid in a cabinet, listening while her mama was raped and murdered."

I felt the air rush from my lungs, and I drew Keisha closer to my chest.

"Then he set the place on fire. Somebody heard Keisha screamin' and ran into that burning apartment. Straight into the fire. He saved her life. But . . . she's never spoken a word since."

I looked at Joe, saw the tenderness in his face as he reached out and touched this precious child. "It was you," I said. "You saved her."

Joe shook his head. "Me?" He chuckled. "Old Samurai Joe? Naw . . . it wasn't me. It was another guy. Man by the name of Anthony Jones."

My heart quickened. "Anthony Jones?"

"Do you know him? He lives next door to the kids. With their mama gone—and who knows what happened with their daddy—the kids had nowhere to go. So he went to his neighbor Mattie. Talked to her, and she took them in. She's a good woman, Miss Mattie is. And she loves these kids."

"I thought she was their grandmother."

"No. Just a good woman. She's got some issues, but she . . . she's the one who stepped up to the plate."

"Because Anthony asked her to."

"Mm-hmm."

Anthony Jones. Could I have been so wrong? Surely a man who would run into a burning house to rescue a child wouldn't kill an innocent man in cold blood. Would he? But if not Anthony . . . then *who?* I'd been convinced enough that I'd broken into his house. Rummaged through his belongings. What kind of person did that make me? Joe talked about pride going before the fall, but how far had I fallen to do something like that?

"Sam?"

I pushed a stubborn tear from my cheek. Rocked a little harder. "I thought . . . I believed Anthony Jones was the man who killed Billy."

"*What?* What would make you think that?"

Joe had been so honest with me. I decided it was time I was just as honest with him. "Joe, I—that night . . . the night I took Keisha to the hospital . . . Haven't you ever wondered what I was doing down there? In the Commons?"

"It crossed my mind, but I figured you'd tell me when you got ready."

I took a deep breath and slowed my rocking. I looked at Keisha and was reminded of the night I held her in my arms, her blood pouring over my hand, seeping between my fingers. "Like I told you, my husband—Billy—was murdered in your neighborhood. In the alley behind Murphy's. *That's* why I was in the Commons that night."

"I thought Billy died three years ago."

"He did." I couldn't look at Joe as I said the rest of what I had to say, so I kept my gaze on the pale color of the hay bales under the moon's light. "The night he got killed, it was raining. It had been raining for days. Last week, when I went back down there . . . to the Commons . . . it was because . . . it had been raining for days and . . ."

"And?"

I couldn't bear to go on with my story, yet I knew I had to. If I was ever going to get past this . . . this *depression* . . . this barrier that stood between me and living again, I had to tell someone—a special someone—the truth about why I had gone into that alley. For whatever reason God had brought Keisha and Macon into my life that night. And through them he'd brought Joe back as well. Together they'd given me the first glimmer of hope and purpose I'd known for three years.

"After what you've told me, Joe . . . after what you've been through, and *survived* . . . And now watching you hooked up to that machine, knowing that at some point . . ."

"Yes, ma'am?"

"I'm ashamed to tell you that I went down to the Commons that night with a .44 Magnum."

My tears began to fall in earnest. I refused to hold them back a minute longer. To do so would split my heart wide open, and surely I would die. But in that moment, by some miracle, my heart wanted nothing more than to go on. To *live*.

I looked at Joe. His face was etched in sorrow and concern. "What were you gonna do with that gun, Sam?"

"I went back to the alley because . . . if that was where some man took Billy's life . . . then that was where I wanted to take my own." I looked at Keisha through my tears—she slept on like the angel she was. "Then I thought . . . I thought I'd found the man who'd done it. Who'd killed Billy. I thought it was Anthony Jones. But . . ." I shook my head.

"Naw, not Anthony. Least, I don't think so."

I drew in a deep breath. Chuckled sarcastically. "Detective Miller was right. Looks like it was a dead-end road."

Joe reached his hand toward me. Slowly. Cautiously. Then he laid it over mine. "Been down a few of those myself. But the one thing I've learned along the way . . ." He moved my hand before drawing Keisha's out from under the blanket. "It's not a dead end," he said, placing her tiny hand in mine, "if it takes you somewhere you needed to go."

Chapter Sixteen

I TOOK KEISHA back inside the house, laid her gently on the floor, and tucked the blanket around her. Then I kissed her forehead. Light from the fireplace danced across her face, showing off the fresh scar left behind from the night we met. In her sleep, she smiled.

When I returned to the porch, Joe was sitting up with his hands on the railing, leaning forward to watch the moon.

"I need to do something out in the barn," I told him. "If you wait, I'll help you back inside."

"Naw, girl. I got it. I'm fine now, really."

"Okay."

I took the steps to the stoop, wrapped my arms around myself, pulling my sweater closer to my body. I could feel Joe watching me, and I turned to look at him over my shoulder. His forearms now rested on the railing. He lifted a hand to wave lightly before dropping his chin onto one of his arms.

I waved back.

Inside the barn I flipped the light switch, waited the few seconds it took for the lights to come on, and then climbed the steps up to the loft, feeling lighter than I had in three years. Upstairs I went straight to the desk and lit a candle I used to keep burning while I worked. I believed it brought me peace and inspiration. Now it would lead me someplace new by destroying what I'd been holding on to for so long. Too long.

I pulled the picture of the man in the red hoodie from under the sketch pad. After studying it for a moment, I sighed. The paper moved as my breath hit it.

Anthony Jones's face did not belong beneath the hood. He'd saved Keisha's life; he hadn't taken Billy's. It had to be true. I had to believe it.

I nodded once, and then dipped a corner of the drawing toward the flame. It caught immediately. I held it until it was nearly consumed, then dropped it onto a tin platter, one of the many items just lying around an artist's studio.

Outside, thunder rolled, catching me off guard. I was feeling better about things, but I wasn't ready for another storm. Like little Firebird, I still hated the rain.

He wanted to know why God gave storms the power to take the sun away. And Mama bird would just smile and say, "You'll understand someday, when you walk on the clouds."

When the sketch had finished burning—when it was nothing more than memory and ashes—I blew out the candle. I heard thunder again, but this time from far off. If there was a storm out there, it wasn't hitting the farm tonight.

I pulled a piece of paper from one of my blank sketch pads, and a charcoal pencil from one of the Mason jars. A new picture had formed in my head. Before I went to bed, I was determined to draw it.

MORNING BIRDS SINGING their wake-up song coaxed me from the most peaceful slumber I'd had in years. I rolled over in bed and looked out one of the three sets of French doors leading to the wraparound balcony outside the second floor. The sun still hid behind the hills, and the eastern sky was a brilliant red.

Red sky at morning, the ancient rhyme played in my mind, *sailors take warning.*

I smiled as I stretched. An old mariner's tale to be sure. Nothing could upset this day. Nothing.

After I'd showered and dressed, I opened the French doors and stepped out onto the balcony. Denise and Brick were already out by the barn with the children. Denise was playing a patty-cake type game with Shannon, one of the older girls. Brick was trying his hand at teaching Macon, Darren, and Bernard the art of roping. Two girls were pushing Chloe in our old wheelbar-row, while Keisha and Peach skipped hand in hand across the yard. When Keisha saw me, she turned and waved. I waved back, amused by her snaggletooth grin and thrilled at seeing the joy on her face.

How different my farm—my home—looked with so many happy young faces running about. I shook my head. No, I decided, Detective Miller was wrong. Very wrong. Good can come out of the Commons.

I was looking at it.

The door behind me opened. I turned, expecting to see Joe, but saw Macon instead.

"Good morning, Macon," I said, welcoming him to the balcony with a smile.

He remained half in and half out the door. "Miss Sam?"

"Yes, sir?"

"I'm hungry."

Macon was *always* hungry. "You don't say? Well, we'll get something to eat on the way back. How does that sound?"

He nodded. "Okay."

I looked again at my guests on the lawn. "Hey, Macon?" I said, turning back to him.

"Yes, ma'am?"

"Where's Joe?"

He shrugged. "I dunno. I guess he's still sleeping. Want me to wake him up?"

I wasn't surprised by this news, seeing as Joe and I had stayed up so late.

"That'd be nice."

Macon nodded. "I'll get 'im."

He started to close the door behind him. "That's okay. Leave it open. I'll come inside in just a minute."

I leaned my shoulder against the post and returned to watching the children. I looked across the yard and the field, up to the multicolored leaves painting the hills. The sky had turned a pristine azure, with only a few white fluffy clouds gracing the blue.

Just then, Denise spotted me from the barnyard. She smiled and waved. I did the same.

"*Miss Sam!*" A distressed cry pierced the moment. "*Miss Sam!*"

Macon!

I turned around and dashed into the house. Macon met me halfway up the stairs. I grabbed him by his shoulders to steady us both. His eyes were wet with tears. "What is it—?"

"It's Joe, Miss Sam! There's blood everywhere!"

I turned him toward the bottom of the staircase. "Go get Brick and Denise. Run!"

Macon made a beeline for the front door, and I headed straight for Joe's room. Macon had left the knotty pine door to the bedroom partially open. I could hear the dialysis machine beeping.

I pushed the door fully open.

Joe lay on the floor, the machine no more than a foot from where his hand was sprawled outward, as though he'd tried to get to it but failed.

Blood pooled thick on the hardwood floor. His blood.

Joe was dying.

AFTER I'D CALLED 9-1-1, I found Brick talking with Macon, suggesting strongly that he not mention anything to the other children. A new level of maturity seemed to rise up in the boy, inching him toward manhood.

Then, while Denise tended to Joe inside, Brick and I loaded the kids onto the bus along with all of their belongings.

Brick said to me, "I'll get them on back to the Commons. Let their mamas and the others know what's going on."

I placed my hand on his arm. "Thank you, Brick." I looked at my watch. "The ambulance should be here any minute."

"Let me get these kids outta here."

I watched the bus drive away. The children hung from the windows, shouting their good-byes and waving frantically. I waved back, forcing myself to remain calm. To appear as though nothing was in the least bit wrong when everything had, once again, turned upside down.

As soon as they were out of sight, I ran back into the house.

Denise knelt over Joe's body with a large towel pressed against the port and catheter. Blood had seeped up to mid-thigh of her jeans. She looked at me, her eyes frantic with worry. "He's still bleeding."

"The ambulance is on its way," I said, joining her, kneeling at Joe's head. "I don't know what else to do . . ."

Denise squeezed my hand with one of hers. "Pray, girl. Pray like you've never prayed before in your life."

"Okay," I said, though I wasn't sure I knew how anymore. There hadn't been many conversations between God and me since Billy died. Last night's talk with Joe had been the closest thing to church I'd attended since the funeral. For three years now part of me had struggled to believe, the old question of how a benevolent God could allow such injustice as Billy's death rearing its head at least once a day. Now, just as I was beginning to sense purpose in my life again—just as I opened the door to Joe's way of thinking—this happens.

"Denise?" I asked. "Do you believe that God is good all the time?"

Her face grew resolute. "I do. In spite of everything I've seen in my life, Sam . . . I believe it. And I believe Joe having this collapse right now—that's in God's timing too. It's in His hands. God knows when the right time for a transplant is. Maybe that time is now."

"What if it isn't?"

"Then God knows best about that too."

Sirens blared in the distance. I looked from this beautiful woman—so full of faith and hope—to the open bedroom door behind me. "Here they come. I'll meet them out front." I stood.

"Denise?" I said, looking down.

"Yeah, baby?"

"You love him, don't you?"

"With everything I got."

Out the front door I saw two ambulances barreling up the road. I stepped on to the front porch and stood behind the same chair Joe had recuperated in the night before. I placed my hands around the back of the chair and squeezed.

It dawned on me then, and I wondered: Had Denise thought I was asking about Joe? Or about God?

DENISE RODE IN the ambulance with Joe, while I followed behind in Billy's truck, breaking every speed law in Davidson County and most of Tennessee. Turned out, the hospital was the same I'd taken Keisha to, so I felt as if I knew my way around. After parking, I found my way to the same waiting area and sat across from the same nurses' station as I had not so many nights before.

Denise met me there. "They're stabilizing him."

"So he's . . ."

She breathed deeply. "He's alive, baby. He's alive."

I fell into her arms, crying.

She squeezed me once before saying, "Girl, I've got to run to the house. Get out of these clothes. I've got blood everywhere. If some of the kids should come up here later, I don't want them to see this."

I nodded. "I'll wait right here. I won't leave, I promise."

She smiled. "I know you won't. I won't be long."

I sat in the same seat I'd occupied the night of Keisha's accident. I stretched to look over the station high-top counter, and then up and down the halls for the nurse who had been so helpful and kind that evening, but she wasn't to be found. I realized then that noon hadn't even arrived, and she was probably a night-shift nurse.

I clutched my purse, pulling it closer than was really necessary. I stared at my feet, just as I'd done that night, acutely aware of the conversations at the nurses' station, the occasional foot traffic up and down the hall. Other than the night Billy died, I had never felt this alone before.

When God's all you got to talk to, God is who you talk to.

I hung my head. "God," I whispered. "I know it's been a while, but . . . my friend Joe. He's very special to me. And I know he's special to You." I thought of Macon and Keisha. Bernard and Peach. And Chloe and Darren and all the others. "He's special to an awful lot of kids too, God. So . . . if it's all right for me to ask this, could You please make sure Joe doesn't die?" I choked. "Because I really don't think I could stand to lose anyone else right now . . ."

I pressed my hands into my face and sobbed.

"Mrs. Crawford?"

I looked up, wiping tears from my cheeks and lashes. A tall doctor dressed in a lab coat and carrying a chart was looking down at me. He was an older man, African-American, with a face that reflected as much concern as kindness. "I'm Dr. Reeves."

"Yes?"

"Mr. Bradford's friend said you would be here when we had news."

I stood. "And? How is he?"

"His body has rejected dialysis. I'm afraid if he doesn't receive a transplant soon, we might lose him."

I pressed my hand to my mouth and closed my eyes against the rest of what he had to say.

What would we do without Joe? What would happen to the kids? To Macon and to Keisha? I dropped slowly back into my seat. "I was hoping for better news," I whispered.

"I understand. But the good news is, he qualifies to be moved up the transplant list. The moment a kidney is available, it's headed our way."

I looked up. "How long will that take?"

"There's no way to know. But I'll be honest with you. We need for it to happen soon."

"And when it does? He'll make it through, right?"

Dr. Reeves shook his head. "From a medical standpoint, there's a small chance with the transplant. But I've been in this business long enough to know that it's not for *me* to say, Mrs. Crawford. We're doing all we can. God handles the rest."

Chapter Seventeen

A HUNDRED AND one questions rose within me, but I couldn't form the words to ask a single one. "Thank you," I finally whispered.

The doctor took a step toward the other side of the hallway, then stopped and turned to look at me. "He's awake. Would you like to see him?"

I stood again. "Yes. That—that would be okay?"

"Absolutely. He's in room 349."

I found my way to 349 and turned slowly into the doorway. The room smelled of alcohol and sickness. Joe lay flat in the bed, an oxygen tube feeding into both nostrils and an IV running to his hand. Machines whirred and beeped around him.

His eyes were closed, the dark circles beneath them an indication of the amount of blood he'd lost. His lips were dry and cracked, and he moaned weakly. My heart broke, both for him and because of my own fear.

A chair had been positioned next to the bed. I eased myself into it and placed my hand over his.

Joe's eyes fluttered open, and he turned his head toward me.

"How are you feeling?" I asked while trying to muster an encouraging smile.

He tried to lean closer to me. I noticed how thick his beard had grown since yesterday. An odd thing to note, but I did so just the same.

"I heard 'em talking," he said, his voice rattling. "They don't think I'll survive the surgery."

I know . . .

"I got no fight left in me, Sam. I think this might be it."

"Shhh. Come on. Don't talk like that."

"Sam, if I . . . I just want you to know something . . . You were an answer to prayer."

Me? "How's that?"

"The night Keisha was hit, I was in bad shape that night. Near as bad as I was . . . when y'all found me. But that night I prayed to God, asking Him to send someone who could help . . . help Denise . . . with the kids. And He sent you. You, Sam. You were God's answer to my prayer, you know that?"

"No, Joe . . . you were an answer to mine."

Joe choked back tears. "Sam, I . . . I love them kids . . ."

I nodded, fighting my own tears. "Do you have time for a story?"

Joe smiled as though amused by such a question. "Well, I sure hope so." He coughed.

"Lay back," I said, gently pushing his shoulder toward the mattress and the pillow.

He flinched as he slowly moved backward, then closed his eyes and waited for me to begin.

I gently squeezed his hand. "Once upon a time . . . there was a little boy who lived in a small village."

A faint smile rose from Joe's lips.

"And he knew he was destined to become a great warrior. But no one else in the village believed it, not even his best friend."

Joe's eyes opened. He cut his eyes at me and nodded.

"Time passed . . . and the little boy and his best friend . . . they grew up, and they grew apart. And like so many of us in life, they lost their way."

Joe turned his head fully toward me.

"It would be many years before Providence would reunite them once again. But when his friend beheld him at last . . . she couldn't believe her eyes . . . for standing in front of her was one of the strongest, most noble, most courageous men she had ever known. A mighty warrior."

Joe nodded again. He understood.

I reached to the floor where I'd dropped my purse and pulled out a folded piece of sketch paper. "I drew this for you . . . last night." I opened it and held it toward Joe, who laid his head back against the pillow again. Sweat beaded across his forehead. I knew he was in great pain, yet his eyes smiled as he studied my drawing.

A new drawing of Samurai Joe, dressed in full samurai regalia. Shoulders back. Chin held high. Proud stance.

Around him were young children, their faces bright and their smiles wide.

Joe took the sketch from my hands. He struggled to speak, first past the physical agony, then through the emotion of seeing himself portrayed so valiantly. Fresh tears formed in his eyes as they did mine. I watched as his tears slipped from his eyes, catching on the oxygen tubing before trailing off.

"These . . . these are my babies," he said.

"I know," I whispered.

"Thank you . . . thank you . . ."

"Thank you."

LATER THAT AFTERNOON, while Joe was resting, I went to the near-empty cafeteria to get a cup of coffee. I sat alone at one of the tables, still hugging my purse, sipping on what was nearly too hot to swallow.

"I'm going to write a new story," I whispered to God. "I'm going to write about Samurai Joe. I'm going to tell the world— one child at a time—about his goodness." I looked out the plate-glass window to an atrium filled with lush plants and a garden fountain. "About *Your* goodness. Because I know . . . I *know* You're not going to take Joe now. I just know it. Not now, when You need him more *here* than You do *there*."

I had to believe then, that three years ago, God needed Billy more than I did or would. That was difficult to swallow. Then again, compared to the needs of these kids . . . well, there was no comparison.

Now, how many you guys comin' up without a father?

No wonder they called him Papa Joe. He was a father to the many who'd not been claimed by their own.

"He's got work to do, God," I spoke into my coffee. "He's got a lot of work to do."

So did I. First, *Firebird*. For Billy. Then . . .

AS I TURNED the corner toward Joe's room, I saw Macon as he ambled into the room, head down, shuffling his feet. He didn't see me. I stepped lightly until I reached the door.

"I need to tell you somethin'," I heard Macon say.

"All right," Joe answered.

I leaned against the door jamb, not wanting to interrupt.

"It's my fault Keisha got hit by the car that night."

"And how's that?"

"I was stealin' some stuff down at Murphy's and got caught. We ran out the back of the store. That security guard Murphy's got down there?"

"Yeah?"

"He chased us through the alley and into the street." Macon's voice rose in distress and guilt. "We was runnin', and then she . . . she . . ."

I heard him sob, choking on his words.

"Aww, come on now." Joe's voice was raspy. "I'm just glad you told me . . . I'm glad you told me."

"I got something I want to show you."

I turned enough to peer into the room. Macon handed Joe a piece of paper. At first Joe held it in his hands, close to his abdomen, not looking at it. His eyes stared straight up at the ceiling, blinking. Then he raised the paper to see what Macon had brought him.

"What's this?"

"My report card."

"Well, look at that. Five A's." Joe cut his eyes to Macon. "Why didn't you show me before?"

Macon sobbed again. "The other boys at school. They say it's stupid to try hard in class. It ain't cool."

Joe brought his hand to Macon's face and cupped it. "Listen to me now . . . *you* are the definition of cool, my man. You are one of the most gifted young men I have ever known." Joe looked again to the report card. "This is *nothing* to be ashamed of."

Macon's head dropped, and his shoulders shook.

"Macon . . . Macon," Joe whispered.

Macon's chin rose.

"I'm so very proud of you."

I placed my hand over my mouth, holding back my own sobs.

"I . . ." Macon began. "I need a favor if you can do it."

Joe chuckled. He wasn't in a position to be doing favors for anyone under the circumstances. "I'll do my best. Tell it to me."

"Would you . . . would you be my dad?"

Joe's chest rose. His eyes closed. When they opened again, they found Macon's. "I wish that I could."

"I read . . . that sometimes . . . other people can give you a kidney. Is that true?"

"Yeah, man. That's true."

"Well, I've been thinking . . . I could give you one of mine."

"Come here," Joe said, coaxing him into his arms.

I turned away, returning to my hiding place, my back against the door jamb. Tears fell softly down my face, tickling my hand, which I held over my mouth. I sobbed without caring who might walk by or who might hear me.

Please, God . . . I prayed. Please.

I RETURNED TO the waiting room until Denise arrived. Together she and I went to Joe's room where Macon had fallen asleep, wrapped in Papa Joe's arms.

"I'll stay with Joe if you want to get Macon home," Denise whispered at the door.

"I'll do that."

I eased Macon awake, winked at Joe, and said, "I'll be back later. I'm going to take this one home."

Macon and I drove back to Mattie's in silence, and I didn't push for conversation. I figured he was emotionally worn out. He sat close, in the middle of the bench seat, shoulders back. The boy had become a man that day. He'd owned up to what had caused his sister's accident. He'd admitted he was a good student. And most importantly, he'd asked a man he always called simply "Joe" to be his "papa."

First thing I noticed when we pulled into the common area was that there seemed to be more trash around the Dumpsters than usual. Hardly seemed possible, but it was true. As if the people who lived there had gotten so used to the debris, they just didn't notice the extra.

Macon walked to where Mattie sat in her usual place outside her front door. As always, she had a lit cigarette between her fingers.

Without a word to Mattie, Macon entered the apartment.

I frowned behind him.

"Thank you for bringing him back," Mattie said.

I shook my head. "He's tired," I said, trying to explain his ill behavior without sharing what I'd overheard in Joe's hospital room. "And maybe a little scared."

"How is Joe?"

"Not good." I sighed. "There is a small chance with a transplant, but he . . . we just have to wait and see if a kidney becomes available."

I thought to say something else, something more hopeful, when the front door opened and Keisha stepped out, showing off her snaggletooth grin.

My heart soared.

She stepped to Mattie, wrapped an arm around her shoulders. Light danced in her eyes.

Mattie chuckled. "I don't know what happened out there at your place, or what you done, but . . ."

Keisha leaned close to Mattie, cupped both hands around her ear and began to whisper.

Mattie's eyes grew bright. "She did? . . . Is that a fact?" She nodded. "I sure will."

I held my breath as Mattie hugged the child.

"She wanted me to tell you . . . thank you for having her out to the farm." Mattie chuckled. "Now look what you done to me," she said, shaking her head. "I told the good Lord I'd quit drinkin' if my baby ever talked again." She chuckled once more, then raised a brow. "Would you like to come inside?"

My mouth probably hung open about three seconds longer than it should have.

"I'd love to," I said.

Keisha held her hand out, and I took it. She led me off the stoop and onto the front porch, then opened the door. As it closed behind me, I heard Mattie chuckle one more time.

The inside of the apartment was bright. Orderly. There wasn't a lot of furniture, and what was there was secondhand. But it was clean. As we entered the living room, Keisha indicated I should close my eyes. After I did, she took me by the hand and led me, shuffling and slightly hunched over, through the house until I heard a door open, squeaking in protest. I assumed it to be her bedroom door.

"Okay," I said, "squeeze my hand when you want me to open my eyes."

I felt a gentle squeeze.

The small room was ablaze with artwork. Brightly colored pages of construction paper with carefully drawn and colored sketches had been taped to nearly ever inch of the pale-yellow walls. Butterflies had been created using puffy paints and buttons. There were glitter-filled flowers so beautifully crafted one could almost smell their fragrance. In the center of one wall was a simple crayon drawing of a box-shaped house, built beneath a smiling sun. Outside its front door Keisha had drawn happy flowers and an impressively rendered bunny.

I inched closer. "Wow," I said, nearly breathless. Everything about this reminded me of my own bedroom at her age. "Did you do all this?"

I looked at her and smiled.

She nodded, clearly proud of her work. Prouder still that I appreciated it.

"It's beautiful. I love it," I said, focusing on a paper with multihued balloons caught together by a giant bow. Underneath the words "I ♥ CANDY" were written in fat letters of pinks and purples. Next to it purple sailboats rocked on a red sea.

Keisha pointed to one of her drawings illuminated by a bed-side lamp whose tilted shade reminded me of the one next to my own bed.

"Do you want me to see something?"

She nodded, drawing me closer.

I pressed a hand to my heart. "Oh, Keisha," I said, stepping nearer to the crayon-drawing of a red-headed woman standing next to a precious little black girl whose hands were raised high. Both were dressed in bright clothes, and both were smiling. They stood in green grass under a shining yellow sun and cheerful blue clouds. "Why, that's us!"

I looked at Keisha. She grinned at me.

I returned to the wall, to the eight-and-a-half-by-eleven pieces of wonder and childhood. Joy washed over me. With our shared love of art, I could see a whole new purpose forming in my life.

Then . . . the air around me stood still.

Staring at me, as if frozen in time, was a drawing—an exact replica of my little Firebird. I grew dizzy. Roaring built to a hurricane-force in my ears, drowning out the rest of the world. My heart beat wildly as I pulled the drawing from the wall, turning it toward Keisha.

Her face had changed from happy to scared. Frightened, no doubt, by the look on my own face. I leaned toward her, pushing the paper close. "Did you draw this?"

She stared at me, unmoving.

"*Keisha?* Where did you see this?" My hands began to shake. As they did, Keisha buried her face into her own. "Keisha! Baby! You have to tell me!"

I was getting nowhere. My gestures and the pitch of my voice had petrified her. I fled from the room, no longer thinking clearly. No longer caring about the feelings of a little girl who I'd made so much progress with only the day before.

Macon sat at the Formica kitchen table, looking at his report card. The same one he'd shown to Joe earlier, the one that had made Joe so proud. I thrust the drawing at him, demanding his attention. His eyes were wide, knowing.

"Where did Keisha see this?" I demanded. "Who showed her how to draw this?"

Macon's eyes darted back and forth over the little oriole, his expression registering that he was more afraid of answering my questions than not.

But I was done playing. I was through with tip-toeing around. Whoever had shown Keisha how to draw Firebird had also taken Billy's copy of my original. And whoever that was had killed my husband.

"*Macon!*"

"It was T, okay? T showed her how to draw it one day. Said it was the only thing he knew how to draw good."

A whimper pushed its way out of my lungs.

I'd been right. All along . . . I'd been right.

Anthony Jones *had* shot Billy. He was the one. And now I had the evidence Detective Miller demanded to make the case against him.

I took two steps back, knowing exactly what I had to do.

Chapter Eighteen

"BABY, *WHAT HAS* gotten into you?"

Mattie's voice came from behind me. I turned around, no longer capable of a rational thought. She looked at me, confusion written on her face, a look that asked, *Why have you come into my home and spoken to my boy in such a way?*

I pressed a hand to my forehead, pushing my hair away from my face, and I looked past her to where Keisha stood, half-hiding, half-peeking around her bedroom door. "I—I have to go," I stammered.

I couldn't get out of the apartment fast enough—my legs seemed to be made of wet dishrags, my boots weighed down with bricks. I stumbled to Billy's truck, my hands shaking so much, it took several attempts to open the door and slide in. As I did, thunder rumbled overhead and sprinkles of rain plopped across my windshield before forming trails toward the wipers.

I threw my purse onto the seat beside me, opened it, and dug around for my phone. Finding it, I flipped it open, my thumb frantically searching the keys for Detective Miller's number. Just as I did—just as I was about to press "send"—I stopped.

Don't call me about this again, you hear me? You're on your own.

I closed my cell phone. My eyes went to the glove compartment. Anger formed in the pit of my stomach, rose to my chest, and gripped my heart. I slowly raised my fingers to the glove compartment's latch. The door fell open, the sound echoing in the truck's cab.

The night of Keisha's accident, I had returned the .44 Magnum to its resting place within the scuffed interior. Since then it had shared the space with an old Bic lighter, the truck's registration papers, and a half-empty box of Tic Tac mints Billy had left behind. I wrapped my fingers around the grip and jerked the gun out. I could see Anthony Jones's apartment building through the rain-drenched windshield, but I could not clearly see his door. Not that it mattered. Opened or closed, home or gone, I was about to right a three-year-old wrong.

I opened the cylinder. The single bullet I'd shoved into one of the chambers was still there, ready and able. But was I?

Ready or not, I no longer cared. If I took the drawing of Firebird to Detective Miller, he'd dally with it. He'd tell me it wasn't enough, that I didn't know what I was dealing with.

My only other choice . . .

I blew out a pent-up breath and climbed out of the truck. I hid the gun under my shirt and shut the door behind me as quietly as possible. Fat raindrops fell on my head, snaking toward my shirt collar as I walked up the cement walkway. Just past the Dumpster and the swing sets, I had my answer: Anthony's front door was wide open. Only the screen door stood between me and justice.

I looked around, but no one was about. The rain had driven them all indoors. A few forgotten articles of clothing hung on the wires stretched across the common area. They grew wetter, and the wires sagged under their weight.

A plastic crate filled with motor oil and a red mechanic's rag sat next to the single step leading up to Anthony's porch. He'd been careless enough to leave behind his work rag in that dark alleyway, and he was foolish enough to leave another one just like it in the open for the wife of his victim to see. I squared my shoulders, reached for the screen handle, and pulled. The door swung open, creaking loudly to announce that a force to be reckoned with had come calling. I dropped my right hand to my side, keeping the barrel of the gun pointed toward the floor, my finger loosely wrapped around the trigger. With the thumb of my left hand, I released the safety.

Nothing about the apartment had changed since I'd last been inside. The rooms were still bathed in shadows, still reeked of motor oil and cigars. I stepped fully into the living room, joining my right hand with my left to hold the gun steady, low and in front of me.

The curtains on the kitchen window had been pushed back, allowing what little bit of overcast daylight could eke past the grime and rust on the screens to penetrate the room. Dishes had been washed and stacked in the drainer. Little was scattered about the countertops—a toaster, a half-empty glass of water, a can opener.

I inched my way toward Anthony's bedroom, walking as quietly as I could in boots on bare tile. At the door to his room, I looked toward the back door. This time, it was tightly shut, cloaking the hallway in a shroud of darkness.

Once inside the bedroom, I rushed to the chest of drawers where Anthony's belt still curled in one corner and a filled ashtray sat in another. In one movement I laid the gun next to the ashtray and jerked open the top drawer. My eyes flew past the newspaper clippings, directly to the cigar box I'd not been able to search the last time I'd been inside this room. I removed the box and placed it next to the gun, pausing a moment to listen for movement inside the apartment.

Nothing. There was only the sound of the rain becoming more insistent, accompanied by the wind's occasional howl outside the building.

I pushed the top of the box open with my thumbs. Inside was a folded piece of paper. I removed it carefully, holding my breath as I pulled the corners open.

My breath caught in my throat.

Firebird . . . my little oriole, staring up at me with Billy's blood splattered across the page. Three-year-old death stains, taunting me.

My hands shook, and I held my breath as I released the drawing. It dropped to rest on top of the open cigar box, sitting next to the gun.

Everything came back to me at once. Camping with Billy. Drawing by the firelight. Reciting my little story to him. His attentiveness.

You keep that drawing for me, you hear?

Sam, you gotta write this. Promise me . . .

I released the breath, taking new ones in past dry, parted lips. "Who are you?"

The quiet voice penetrated the cadence of the rain and the sound of my own ragged breathing. I spun around, sweeping the gun off the dresser and gripping it with both hands. My arms extended, I pulled the hammer back.

Anthony Jones's eyes grew large as the gun's chamber clicked into place. I stared at him, determined not to be afraid, unwavering in my assurance that this man had killed Billy.

Without taking my eyes from his, I reached behind me and grabbed the drawing of Firebird with my left hand. "I'm Samantha Crawford," I said. In spite of my resolution, my voice quivered slightly. I held the paper between him and me. "You killed my husband."

He took a step into the semidarkness of the room. "How'd you find me?" He sounded genuinely shocked, as though he'd never expected this moment to come.

I grabbed the gun with both hands again, showing him I meant business. "Don't!"

Little Firebird slipped out of my hand and floated to the floor, landing at the toes of my boots.

Anthony raised his hands. Thick chest muscles strained beneath the gray ribbed tank he wore tucked into a pair of belted jeans. "You don't wanna do that, now." He slowly lowered himself to one knee, hands splayed, never taking his eyes off mine. "You need to hear what I gotta say to you . . . 'cause your husband . . . he wanted me to tell you something . . ."

What . . . ? Had Billy whispered a message for me to his killer mere seconds before he died?

Both knees came to the floor and Anthony straightened his back as though to make a point. I kept the gun pointed at his head. "You ain't gonna believe me." He blinked once, then swallowed, his Adam's apple bobbing slowly up, then down. "But I need you to try . . ."

I didn't answer. Couldn't answer. I could only barely take in his words. Guilty or not, he knew the details of the last minutes of Billy's life. Details I wanted to hear. I *needed* to hear.

"You already know I was there . . . It was raining that night. A hard rain. A break had come in it, and I was headin' over to my cousin's house. Thought I'd have enough time to get there on foot before it started raining again, but . . ." He took several breaths, his eyes never leaving mine. "I got just about to Murphy's when the bottom fell out again. I was wearing . . . I had on this red hoodie . . ."

My chest constricted.

The killer wore a red hoodie . . .

"I've seen it," I said. "Seen it the day you got on to Macon for putting it on."

Anthony's eyes turned sad. "Macon. That boy . . . he don't know what's good for 'im."

I didn't want to talk about Macon. I wanted to talk about Billy. "What happened outside Murphy's?"

"I stood up under the awning, hands shoved in my pockets, madder than a hornet that I was stuck there. It was dark all around. No lights coming from inside, none from the outside either. Then all of a sudden I hear this electrical buzzing and the lights come on.

"Next thing I know, your husband comes walking around from the corner of the alley. He's more drenched than me, if you can imagine." A faint smile crossed Anthony's lips. When I didn't return it, he continued. "He was taking off his hard hat—I remember, it was white—tucked it under his arm as he passed by. He nodded, like he knew me.

"I nodded back. I knew he didn't belong around the Commons, but his eyes . . . they were kind."

Tears burned my own eyes. Anthony's image glistened before me. I raised the gun a tad higher. "Go on."

"Your husband knocked on Murphy's door, and old Murphy opened it. I could see him, but he couldn't see me. Or if he could, he didn't notice. He looked at your husband standing there and said, 'My man, you did it.'

"'Just the transformer,' your husband said.

"'Well, I thank ya kindly, anyway.'

"Your husband asked if he had any coffee going. Was probably chilled to the bone."

That knowledge pained me more than I could have imagined it would.

"Old Murphy said, 'I can put some on. Won't take a second to start it.' He moved on back into the store, but Billy—your husband—he turned and looked at me. 'You live around here?' he asked me. 'Do you need a ride?'

"I told him I was heading over to my cousin's as soon as the rain let up. Your husband looked at the sky, scoping out the weather. He said, 'May be a while. Can I get you anything?' He looked at Murphy's like he would have bought me something, and he didn't even know me."

"He would have," I whispered.

"I told him no. I mean, I wasn't used to white guys from other parts of town offerin' to buy me anything. But he wasn't in that store five minutes before he came back out with a sandwich and a cup of coffee."

It seemed to me Anthony was struggling now. Not because he wasn't sure of his story, but because Billy had encouraged him somehow, the way he managed to touch everyone he ever came into contact with.

Still . . . Anthony had killed him. Even this show of kindness, he had gunned Billy down. *For what?*

"He . . . he sat with me for an hour in that rain. And we talked about a lotta things. The rain let up a little, and he said he had to get back home. He'd . . . he'd told me all about you. That you was a children's book writer and . . ."

My breath jerked out of my body as though I'd been kicked in the chest. The gun wavered in my hand. Anthony's eyes shifted, telling me he saw it too.

"His truck wouldn't start. I heard it, the engine trying to turn over. So I went into the alley, and I helped him fix it. He'd done something nice for me—it was the least I could do."

The least . . .

"I always been good with cars. After I got it running, he walked with me back to the front of the store and we talked some more under the awning. He said he wanted to see me again. Said he'd be back the next day . . . we'd get another cup of coffee and a sandwich or something. I said the next one was on me."

I blinked. Angry tears spilled down my cheeks, clearing my vision. My finger was still wrapped loosely around the trigger.

"He turned to head on back down the alley, and I decided the rain weren't never gonna clear up. I was wet enough, I may as well walk on to my cousin's. I got about twenty feet to the other side of the street when I turned to look over my shoulder. I could see Murphy through the window. He was mopping. Had headphones on, and I could see he was singin' with the music."

Anthony's brows drew together. "No sooner had I turned around than I heard two gunshots coming from the alley."

A groan escaped between my lips as though the bullet had penetrated my heart just as it had Billy's.

"I ran to the corner. Your husband lay on the ground, and this shadowy figure in a dark-blue hoodie was bent over him, rummaging through Billy's pockets.

I yelled, and the man looks up just as this flash of lightning shot across the sky."

"Did you . . . see his face?"

Anthony barely nodded. "Yes, ma'am."

"Who?" I couldn't get the rest of the words to come, so I repeated it again. "Who?"

"Don't know. Some white dude with a crooked nose. Never seen the man before or since."

My arms grew tired, and the gun barrel began to dip slowly toward the floor as my finger eased around the trigger guard.

"The man dropped a wallet. He took three shots at me. I figured later he must not have had but five bullets 'cause he took off running after that." Anthony shook his head. "He was cuttin' around the other end of the alley when I got to Billy. And Billy, he was struggling, trying to reach the wallet."

Fresh tears followed the old ones, these hotter than the ones that had already dripped off my chin and onto Anthony's bedroom floor.

Anthony Jones ran his tongue over dry lips. "I knelt down beside him. 'Gonna be all right, man. Gonna be okay,' I told him. 'I'll go get help.' But Billy shook his head, still struggling to get to that wallet.

"'You want this?' I said. He nodded, and I got it for him. He scratched at it, like he was trying to open it. So I helped him, and he took out this folded piece of paper. Grabbed hold of my hand, pressed the paper into it, and pulled himself up so I could hear him. I knew . . . I knew it was bad. Blood was spillin' outta his mouth, so I knew. And I knew whatever he had to say, it was too important for me to leave him there, even to go get help."

"What? What did he say?" I choked out.

"He said, 'Tell Sam . . . tell Sam . . . *Always* walk on the clouds.'"

The weight of fresh grief laid itself against my back, pressing my shoulders forward. The gun now hung loosely at my side. With my thumb, I slipped the safety into place, though there was still one more thing I had to know . . .

"I knew they'd blame me," Anthony continued, "so I ran. I heard later they were looking for a man in a red hoodie with a red mechanic's rag. I'd used one of the rags I always kept in my pocket when I worked on his truck. I figured it must have fallen out when I was kneelin' over him."

I stared straight ahead, at Anthony's black, tender eyes. What I'd seen in them before . . . was somehow different now. Like Macon coming clean with Joe, Anthony had finally been able to tell Billy Crawford's wife the truth. It had set him free.

"Since that night," Anthony went on, his eyes welling with tears, "I ain't never been the same. Because of your husband. Because of our time together."

Me either . . .

"Is that all . . . all he gave you?" I asked.

"No, ma'am." Still kneeling, his hand slowly stretched toward the drawing. Reverently, it seemed, he picked it up and handed it to me. Unable to hold me up a second longer, my legs folded. I knelt before him, accepting the token of Billy's final gift to me.

I already knew about the drawing. "I don't understand," I whispered.

Anthony had dropped back on his haunches. As my eyes met his, he leaned forward. When his hands touched mine, he forced them to flip the drawing over where I could see, even in the dim light, that something had been taped to the underside.

It was a two-dollar bill.

Chapter Nineteen

I RETURNED TO the hospital the following day. Just as the automatic door slid open before me to allow me entrance, I heard someone call my name. Turning, I saw Denise running up the walkway toward me and carrying a bouquet of autumn flowers.

"Hey," I said. "Any news?"

"Not that I know of. I called up to the nurses' station before I left the house, and they told me that he held his own during the night."

I pointed to the door. "I was just heading up."

"Wait," she said. She opened her purse and pulled out an envelope. A name had been scribbled in cursive across the front center.

Sam.

"Joe wanted me to give you this. He gave it to me last night before I left. He really struggled to write it, so . . ."

I looked down at the plain letter-sized envelope, rubbing my palm across it. "What is this?"

She smiled. "I don't know, baby. I'm just the messenger. But whatever it is, it was important to him to write it."

On both sides of the hospital's front door sat benches of wood and wrought iron, each surrounded by thick, cherry-red, Knock Out rose bushes. I motioned to one of the benches. "I'll sit out here and read it," I said, not willing to wait to find out what Joe had written.

Denise squeezed my arm. "I'd say it's a good day for it." She turned to go inside.

"Denise, wait . . ."

Her brow raised. "What's wrong?"

"Do you have a minute?"

She stole a glance at the flowers, as though they would die if she didn't get them in water soon enough, but then smiled. "For you? Of course."

We sat together on one of the benches. I crossed my legs, shifting my knees in her direction. "I wanted to ask you . . . yesterday, I asked about . . . well, about loving him. But I didn't really say which 'him' I meant. Joe or God."

Her broad smile spread across her face. "I figured that out yesterday. The truth is, I love them both." Her hands clasped mine. "I believe God brought Joe into my life for a reason. Maybe two, maybe three. I don't know. For sure, to minister to these kids, which is the easy part. Spend five minutes with them, and your heart is completely arrested. But maybe . . . maybe, God has more in mind." Her almond-shaped eyes shot heavenward.

I saw the same look on her face as I'd worn when I first met Billy and every day of our lives together thereafter. Knowing now how Denise felt about Joe gave me something of the same sense of wonder and excitement.

"What attracted you to him—to Joe—in the beginning?"

Her eyes cut playfully in my direction. "You mean other than those muscles of his?"

We laughed together, and she squeezed my hands again. "Seriously, at first I only thought of him as a friend. Then I got to know his heart. It's the warmest of any person I've ever known. His desire to help those babies in the projects, to rise above his situation in life and to thank God for what most men would have cursed God for, is nothing short of amazing."

I nodded. Amazing, yes. And humbling. For three years I'd wallowed in my own grief, but Joe had found light in the shadows. Hope in the midst of despair and poverty.

Denise sighed deeply, drawing me back. "I just have to wait for God to show Joe whether or not I'm supposed to be more than a friend." She took the flowers in one hand and held them up. "If we get past all this."

I leaned closer. "We will, Denise. You'll see. I just know we will."

After she'd walked into the lobby and disappeared around the corner to where the elevators were located, I uncrossed my legs and tore open the envelope. A nurse pushing a man in a wheelchair rolled past, and I watched until they reached the semicircular sidewalk, turned right, and continued on.

Resting against the ornate back of the bench, I removed a piece of simple stationery from the envelope and read:

Dearest Sam,

You'll never know what it's meant to be seeing your face again and reuniting with that lovely little red-headed girl who welcomed a stranger as a friend. It's been hard to see those once hopeful eyes now only carrying the pain of a shadowed life. Well, I know those eyes all too well. But with pain comes a new way of seeing things. See, at the edge of death, I've never felt more alive, because I know I've done what I was created to do, to love these kids. I also knew that if anything happened to me, Denise couldn't do it alone, and then you came along. That wasn't without reason, Sam. Maybe these kids can help you find your way again. Like they did me.

Remember that story you wrote about God and the sparrow? I heard you say you didn't believe it anymore and that's okay. He's patient. I'm proof of that. Whatever happens, I have peace and I only want the same for you. Find your stride, Sam. Share your stories. They matter. Live. Breathe. And find a way to believe again.

Love,

Joe

I read the letter again and again, all the while vaguely aware of the constant opening and closing of the hospital door. Of visitors and medical personnel passing in and out. Of the breeze that slipped through the covered walkway, and of the light, spicy scent of the roses nearby. But it wasn't until I felt someone touch my shoulder that I looked up.

A young nurse dressed in blue scrubs gazed down at me. Her blue-black hair had been caught in a careless ponytail. Her Asian eyes were both compassionate and serious. "Mrs. Crawford?"

I folded the letter while keeping my eyes on her. "Yes?"

"A lady named Denise Lyles asked me to come down here and get you. They're taking Mr. Bradford to surgery right now."

I stood. "What? *Right now?*"

"Yes, ma'am."

I glanced at the automatic glass door, hope springing in my chest. "They got a kidney for him so soon?"

She smiled. "Yes, ma'am. They found a match from a donor bank."

"Do I have time before . . . ?"

She shrugged as she shook her head. "I'm not sure. But you can try for it. Do you know where his room is?"

"Yes." I pushed the letter back into the envelope and shoved it into my purse. "Thank you so much!"

I brushed past her and entered the lobby, walking quickly to the elevators. When the doors didn't open fast enough, I looked around for the stairs. Spotting a door under a neon sign, I dashed over, yanked the door open, and took the stairs, two at a time. When I reached the third floor, I was both winded and anxious. I forced myself to breathe normally, not wanting to appear too worried on the chance I happened to make it before Joe was taken to surgery.

But when I stepped into his room, I realized I was too late. His bed was gone, as were some of the machines he'd been hooked up to since his arrival. Denise's handheld floral arrangement had been tossed onto the window sill. The emptiness of it all should have caused me sorrow—I had not had a chance to say good-bye. But I was too stunned to feel regret. Since my departure the day before, the walls around the room had been overwhelmed by get-well cards taped to the walls. Dozens of them. Some store-bought. Most handmade. Lovingly penned and crafted by little hands. Children's hands.

These . . . these are my babies.

I stepped reverently toward the nearest card. It was made from orange construction paper and written in black crayon. GET WELL SOON PAPA JOE, it read. It was signed by Latisha.

Another, on bright yellow paper with a luscious red strawberry drawn in the center, read, I ATE A STRAWBERRY TODAY AND THOUGHT OF YOU.

There were so many others. I took the time to study each one, noting the love that had gone into every petal of every flower, every rainbow color of every fat balloon.

I felt my brow furrow as something occurred to me. In these cards the sun was always smiling, the clouds were always happy, the flowers always bloomed. Not a single image indicated that it was drawn by an unhappy child.

What a glaring difference from the drawings that had hung over my work desk the past three years.

I lived on a beautiful farm, in a house large enough to get lost in, full of expensive, handcrafted cabinets and doors and cushy pieces of furniture. I never worried where my next meal was coming from. Never fretted over whether or not the electric bill would get paid.

I had been given the opportunity, every day, to watch the sun come up in majesty and go down in splendor. I could stand out on my balcony or front porch and breathe in the scent of fresh hay and green grass—not garbage overflowing from Dumpsters that were emptied too rarely.

Yet for the past three years my drawings had been nothing but dark. Shadowy men in red hoodies. Blood spilled in alleyways. Red rags tossed along the asphalt.

Because of Joe—because of *God's* working in Joe's life—these kids had looked past the obvious of their surroundings to see all kinds of possibilities. Meanwhile I had ignored life's gifts, choosing to dwell only on the sinister, painful parts of this world.

I'd spent so much time dwelling on the murderous dragon, I'd nearly forgotten the blessings of the years I'd spent in the company of the knight.

Two machines that had been switched off and disconnected from Joe now sat silent, their wires tangled in the legs of an empty visitor's chair wedged between them. I lowered myself onto the orange vinyl, imagining the flurry of activity that must have taken place to get Joe out of the room and into surgery. As if I had not cried enough in the past few days, tears again found their way to the corners of my eyes and trailed down my cheeks. I slowly covered my face with my hands and drew in a deep breath.

"I'm so sorry, God," I whispered. "I'm so sorry. I've wasted precious time. Your precious time, another one of Your gifts to me.

Thrown away. Tossed aside like the trash littering the Commons. But I know now. I understand. I get what You've always had for me: a purpose and a plan. And I also know now that sometimes those plans mean losing the ones we love the most . . . and giving them back to You."

You'll understand when you walk on the clouds someday.

I swallowed hard. "Billy was the best thing in my life," I prayed. "I didn't think I could breathe without him. And to tell you the truth, I never saw the day coming when I'd have to. But here I am. Without him. And I'm still breathing because . . . I'm still here. And You're still here, like You've always been, walking beside me."

No storm could take the sun away. The sun was always shining.

I rested my elbows on my knees, and my hands fell limp between them. My shoulders hunched as I continued, "But now there's Joe . . . God, I know You make these choices, but I'm asking—I'm begging, if I have to—heal Joe. By whatever medical science is available and by whatever brilliance You have placed in those men and women who are standing around him right now, heal him. Bring him back to us whole. Whole and healthy. So he can continue to walk the path You've laid before him. And do Your will. Your work."

It's up there waiting for you today. But you have to go see it for yourself.

I dried my tear-streaked cheeks with my fingertips. "But no matter what," I said, "I'm Yours." I shook my head. "I won't doubt You again. Or Your love. Not ever. Not ever . . ."

I looked up, past where Joe's bed had been, to the wall where one of the cards caught my eye. It had been signed by Keisha, and it featured a bird, painted blue, soaring high over a line of pink, fluffy clouds. So much like my little Firebird.

All he needed was a little walk on the clouds.

I guess that was all I needed too.

I WASHED MY face in the small sink in Joe's room, then dried it using rough paper towels from the dispenser hanging nearby. A glance in the mirror told me I looked about as bad as I suspected I would. My hair, which I'd tied back in a braid earlier that morning, had come loose around my face. There were dark circles under my eyes, and the green of my irises looked washed out.

My skin, devoid of any makeup, looked pale beyond the usual.

I was tired . . . exhausted really. And yet . . . I felt more alive than I had in a long, long time.

In the mirror's reflection I saw Denise's flowers, still laying on the window sill. I found a plastic cup from Joe's bedside table, filled it with water, inserted the flowers, and propped them up against the corner of the window.

Then I went to find the surgical waiting room. Perhaps Denise and the others would be there. After all, an organ transplant was a long and complicated surgery, and I didn't want to wait here alone.

I rode the elevator to the fifth floor and followed the signs. When I turned the corner, I saw Mattie sitting on a small sofa. Macon and Keisha sat with her, one on either side. As their heads turned toward the sound of my boots clomping against the terrazzo flooring, my eyes locked with Keisha's.

This poor child. The last time I'd seen her, I'd yelled at her. If the downturn of her sweet, pink lips was any indication, she'd stopped talking again. Because of me. Because I'd grown so focused on the *wrong* things that I hadn't taken care of the right ones.

Mattie's arms were around both children. As she stood, they stood with her. Concern colored the features of her face, and it seemed to me Macon had aged another decade. No wonder the boys in the projects didn't make it past twenty-one. By the time most of them had reached twelve, they'd survived more than most men did in fifty years.

I wanted to get my apology out of the way first thing, so our relationships might begin to mend. But as soon as I came face to face with Mattie, she spoke before I had the chance.

"T came by last night and told me 'bout what happened to your husband. I'm so sorry, child."

I shook my head. "No. I'm sorry. I didn't mean to bring trouble to you or your home."

Her eyes grew wide with compassion. "Oh, you no trouble, baby." Her brow rose. "You family."

And with that, she drew me into her arms.

She smelled of sweet tobacco and gardenias, faith and forgiveness.

I dropped my head on her shoulder and, as I did, I felt Keisha's and Macon's arms wrap around the two of us. I heard Macon's sniffles and sensed his tears.

Yes, indeed. We *were* family.

Chapter Twenty

CEMETERIES ARE STRANGE places. Gardens of stone, I've heard them called. The first word sounds so pretty, the other . . . so cold. The reality is, cemeteries are stretches of grassy plain punctuated by concrete and gravel. This is where we lay our loved ones when a life is no more and the body is all that remains.

At first, immediately after a loss, we visit frequently. As months and years go by . . . not as often. We lay flowers near the headstone, often trading out old floral arrangements for fresh ones. We kneel, pull at weeds, and talk for a moment or two before realizing we aren't really speaking to our loved ones at all. We're just saying what we would have said if they were there with us.

And maybe, for a few moments, they are.

Six weeks after Joe's surgery, I stopped by the only floral shop in my little farming community. There I purchased a single long-stemmed red rose. I laid it beside me on the seat of Billy's old Ford and then drove to the cemetery just north of town. The day was clear, the sky a most amazing blue. White clouds dotted across it as though the scene had been painted by a child. The trees along the horizon had lost most of their leaves, though the grass on the hillsides not yet turned fully brown. But the old would soon give way, to be blanketed by winter and lie in wait for the rebirth of spring.

After parking the truck, I picked up the rose and walked to an ornate headstone, the one I'd visited so many times before. As I stood before it, a peaceful breeze picked up my hair. The red strands billowed before settling around my shoulders and across the thick plum-colored sweater I'd worn to keep out the autumn chill.

Hey, purty lady.

I laid the rose at the base of the headstone. "Hey, cowboy." I swallowed, waiting for something. But, as with every other visit, I didn't know what.

"I wish," I finally said, "that you could see me today." I smiled playfully. "I'm all dressed up. Got my hair brushed out the way you always liked it, and I'm even wearing makeup again." I folded my hands together. "But who knows? Maybe you *can* see me after all. Maybe you already know that I . . . I've started living again."

The sound of tires crunching over gravel caught my ear, pulling my attention to one of the driveways leading into the cemetery. A silver-toned Chrysler rolled slowly to a stop. I watched as Denise got out of the driver's seat and Joe exited the passenger's. He carried a bouquet of orange and yellow mums clustered with wild daisies.

He looked handsome, dressed in a dark-blue long-sleeved shirt and dress jeans. More than handsome—he looked healthy. And Denise . . . she was always a beauty. But today . . . well, she just looked so extraordinarily *happy*.

She joined Joe on his side of the car, and they clasped hands before walking toward me, both of them smiling. I turned fully to greet them but said nothing.

For a while we stood together in silence, looking down at Billy's name, his date of birth, the date of his death. Forever reminders that he had been taken too soon. Joe eventually laid the flowers next to my single rose, then straightened. Strong. Without wincing or faltering. Joe was doing well.

"You almost done with your project?" he asked me then.

"I am. It won't be much longer. The hardest part was chasing the dust bunnies out of the loft."

Not that I'd expected it to be difficult. The writing, the drawing had been easy as when I was a child. After so many years Firebird had come to life. On the page. Inside of me.

"Well, when it's done, we're gonna throw a celebration like you've never seen before."

I laughed lightly. "Best that we wait until after my publisher sees it and decides whether or not it's publishable."

Denise laid her head against Joe's shoulder. "Keisha has been working hard on the celebration banners, so . . ." Her smile was broad, infectious. "I suggest that publisher of yours take note."

I laughed again. "I'll tell them."

I glanced down at the grave. "Billy really wanted me to tell this story," I said, my words whispery soft. "If nothing else, one day I'll be able to say to him that I did."

Joe kissed Denise's forehead. "Following through, girl. That's what it's all about."

"What about you?" I asked him, looking at Denise. "You following through?"

Denise extended her left hand in my direction. A small diamond winked in the midmorning sun. "I guess he is," she said.

"Well, I guess so," I said before hugging them both.

One Year Later

CHRISTMAS SEASON WAS, once again, my favorite time of year, and preparations had been made during one of the many farm outings we'd scheduled for the kids. With the help of Macon, Bernard, and a few of the other boys, I'd brought all the lights and decorations down from the attic. Joe and Brick had supervised the young men stringing the lights around the outside of the house and barn, while inside, Denise oversaw the baking of cookies. Keisha, Mattie, and I were responsible for decorating the windows and doors and hanging four Christmas stockings from the fireplace mantel. The stockings had been handmade by Mattie the year before, knitted with love, each finished with a name carefully stitched at the top.

Keisha.

Macon.

Mattie.

Sam.

For the second year in a row, my new family would be waking up on Christmas morning at the farm, with me. Just as I hoped they always would.

The scent of vanilla and cinnamon filled the house, made

warmer still by the crackling of a fire Joe had lit in the fireplace. I pulled back one of the living room curtains, just as I had so many years before, when I'd waited for Billy to come up the driveway. Peering at the sky, I said, "Clouds out there are threatening snow."

From the kitchen Denise laughed. "No, baby. They're promising snow. We're gonna have a white Christmas, I just know it."

I glanced at a group of our girls, who carefully laid the tree ornaments on the kitchen table. Later that night we'd all drink hot cocoa, listen to traditional Christmas carols (at my insistence), and trim the tree. I don't know who was more excited, the children or me.

I started to turn away from the window, but froze at the sound of a truck coming up the driveway. I turned, anxious. Even after all these years, I sometimes expected to see Billy. But instead of an old blue-and-white Ford Custom Cab, it was a white cargo truck with two-toned lettering that read *FedEx*.

"Oh, my gracious," I said. "I bet I know what this is."

I went out to the front porch and waited for the burly delivery man to bring a box up the steps and deposit it at my feet. "Need any help gettin' this inside?" he asked.

Macon and the others had already begun to climb the steps to the porch. "No sir," I said with a grin. "I think I've got all the help I need."

After I signed for the delivery, he tipped his hat and said, "Merry Christmas."

"Merry Christmas to you too."

Joe walked up, saying, "Kids? Give it up!"

"Merry Christmas," they bellowed, jumping up and down as they did so. The driver laughed and tipped his hat one more time.

"Who wants to help me get this in the house so we can see what's inside?" I said.

Macon swept the box up in his newly muscled arms and headed inside.

Everyone followed. I said, "Put it over there by my rocker, Macon." Joe tossed a pocketknife my way as I sat in the rocker. I told the kids to gather around, and as I slit the seal on the box, the flaps popped open.

Joe and Denise sat on the sofa and were joined by Brick and Mattie. All around me, the children gathered on the floor and in the occasional chair. Keisha found her way to my lap, climbing into it as naturally as if she were my own child.

By now I was holding up the prize in all its glossy wonder. One of fifty copies of Firebird. "Look at this," I whispered to Keisha.

I opened the cover to the first page. I looked at the children. "Y'all ready to hear a story?"

They cheered in affirmation.

"Once upon a time," I read, "there lived a little baby oriole bird. His mama called him Firebird on account of his amazingly beautiful orange feathers. Now Firebird just lived for the sunshine. He would bask in that sunshine for hours."

I turned the page. "Your turn," I whispered to Keisha.

"But when the rains would come," she read out loud, "he would go complain to his mama. He wanted to know why God gave storms the power to take the sun away. And Mama bird would just smile and say, 'You'll understand when you walk on the clouds someday.'"

I glanced toward Joe, whose wife sat tucked under his arm at the end of the sofa. They beamed with pride. Denise rolled her head back against Joe's arm and laughed in that way she was known to do—silently, yet with such fullness of joy.

Mattie's clear eyes sparkled in concurrence.

"Very good," I said to Keisha. "Very, very good."

THAT SPRING I received a call from Denise wanting to know if I could come to the house to help with snack time and homework. I'd been working on my next book—the one about Samurai Joe and his loyal apprentices—when the call came. I told her that her timing was perfect and that I'd gladly take a break and drive into town.

"Would you mind terribly stopping at Murphy's? Picking up some peanut butter and jelly for sandwiches? We're out, and it would surely save me some time."

"Be happy to do that too," I said.

An hour later I was pulling up to the curb outside of Murphy's, a place I'd grown accustomed to dashing into for last-minute items Joe and Denise—and sometimes Mattie—needed. But this time I paused before reaching the door.

In the window someone had taped a two-dollar bill under a handwritten sign that read: PASS IT ON.

After a moment or two of staring, I went on inside. The scent of fresh ground coffee wafted through the store, and I thought, as always, of Billy and of the night he'd brought coffee to Anthony Jones. "Hey, Murphy?" I called as my sandaled feet crossed the unpainted wood floor between shelves of stocked grocery items.

"Hey, Miss Sam!" he hollered back.

His voice had come from the back of the store. I followed it to where two of the local old-timers were engaged in an intense card game. Murphy's back was to me. He peered over the shoulder of one of the men, checking out his cards, but cast a glance my way once I was close enough to talk without shouting.

I pointed to the front of the store. "What's up with the two-dollar bill?"

"It was T's idea," he said. "He's got one up at the shop where he works, and there's one over at the restaurant where Mattie's been working ever since she got herself sobered up, thanks to you. I even saw one stuck in a cab's windshield the other day."

There's enough love to go around, Sam. You just have to share it.

My fingertips came to rest at the base of my throat. "Are you serious?"

"Yes, ma'am. You look around. You'll see 'em all over the Commons. Wouldn't be surprised if they aren't all the way to the county buildings by now."

Maybe, I thought, to Detective Miller's office.

"Isn't that something?" I said.

"Your husband, see, he was here one night. Just one. Got the lights turned on for me, but in his own way he's turned on a light that cain't be turned off. And cain't nothing outshine love, Miss Sam. Not a thing I know of."

"Not a thing I know of, either," I said. "Not a single thing."

I purchased the peanut butter and jelly and left the store, but not before deciding to drive over to the service station where Anthony worked. He wasn't there, but sure enough there was the same PASS IT ON sticker holding a two-dollar bill against the glass window of the station's convenience store.

I headed on over to Joe and Denise's. As soon as my feet hit the pavement of the sidewalk, I heard cheering coming from the backyard. I was late. The kids were already there. In my efforts to see Anthony—to thank him—I'd lost time.

I hurried around the side of the house.

As soon as I turned the corner to the backyard, everyone—Joe, Denise, Mattie, the children, some of the mothers, and Anthony—yelled, "Surprise!"

They wore colorful party hats, and the tables were covered in paper tablecloths with giant balloons along the edges. Each table held a centerpiece made of birthday balloons. Macon stood front and center, holding a cake loaded with lit candles.

Anthony started the chorus of "Happy Birthday," with Joe accompanying on his saxophone. When the song was over, the children chanted, "Make a wish! Make a wish!"

I squeezed my eyes shut . . . took in a deep breath . . . and I blew.

THE FOLLOWING WEEK Cricket and I took an early morning pleasure ride around the fields and through a trail in the woods. After returning, I removed her tack, then let her walk freely outside the barn with Penny. Together they grazed on grass and hay, content in the world in which they lived.

Just as I was.

I then went upstairs to the loft to make some final touches on *The Tale of Samurai Joe*. I had worked on it for about an hour when the first rumblings of thunder rolled overhead.

I chose to ignore the approaching storm.

A few minutes later Cricket and Penny's neighs came from below, answered by Maggie's moo. Within seconds heavy rain pelted the roof of the barn, the cadence sounding like a marching army. I looked around, suddenly aware of how dark the loft had become. Only the light from the lamp on my desk held back the shadows.

I slid off the stool where I perched while working, and I walked over to the wide loft windows. I pushed them open. Outside the rain turned the world's colors to magnificent hues. Just above the horizon, dark clouds hung thick in the gray sky. I blinked slowly and smiled, because I knew . . . I knew . . . that high above those clouds, the sun continued to shine.

Constant and unchanging.

On a whim I climbed down the stairs and threw open the barn doors. Stepping into the barnyard, I held my arms straight out before me, allowing the rain to cup in my hands before spilling over. I tilted my face upward toward where I knew the sun still shone. I closed my eyes and felt the rain wash over me, plastering my hair to my scalp. And I breathed in the glory of it all.

I smiled as my hands reached heavenward slowly, slowly, until—in my heart—I burst up through the clouds and took a walk on them.

LIFE IS SO beautiful. So full of magic and possibilities. When Billy died, I thought that my story had come to an end. But I was wrong.

Joe helped me to find something I had lost along the way. Something I'd once believed so strongly: that the storms of life were bound to come, but maybe even in the storms, in the loneliest times of all, you're never really alone.

Love is the most powerful thing on earth. I've seen what it can do. And it can do amazing things. Sometimes I imagine a world where everyone knows of a love that's unconditional. And what a beautiful world it is.

I think Billy had it right, that there truly is enough love to go around. All you have to do is share it.

What if God's love is like the sun, constant and unchanging? What if you woke up one day and realized . . . nothing can take that away?

THIS STORY WAS inspired by actual events from the life of Papa Joe Bradford. Papa Joe and Denise Bradford's ministry began with one child and a piece of candy. Today they are committed to partnering with others to share God's love in a way that changes the lives of children who are terribly at risk due to circumstances beyond their control. To find out how you can help, or to learn more about Papa Joe and the ministry of Elijah's Heart, visit www.papajoe.org or www.elijahsheart.com.

Right now more than 113,000 people are waiting for an organ transplant. Of those, eighteen will die every day waiting. One organ donor can save up to eight lives. One person's donation saved the life of Papa Joe Bradford, who has gone on to change the lives of many others. Whose life might you save? For more information on becoming an organ donor, go to www.organdonor.gov.

Acknowledgments

I CANNOT THANK all the good people at Harbinger Media and B&H Publishing enough for trusting me with this story. Thank you to Bill Reeves of Working Title Agency for knowing I would be a good fit. Thank you to Jonathan Clements, my extraordinary and fabulous agent. Thank you to my editor, Julie Gwinn. What fun to finally get to work with you!

Thank you to my critique partner, Shellie Arnold. You make me think harder and feel more deeply than I like to. (I always cry!) But in the end the product shows the effort. You are amazing.

David Webb, you are "da man" when it comes to editing. What a great team we made! "Udderly ridiculous" is what we are. Every writer should be so blessed to work with you at least once.

Thank you, Papa Joe and Denise Bradford, not only for sharing your story with the world, but for sharing it with me. Thank you for what you do for these kids. My heart soars every time I think about it. You are an inspiration to so many. You are an inspiration to me.

Thank you to my huggy hubby, who has supported me 150 percent in this "writing and publishing thing." Next to Jesus, you are my greatest gift from God.

Sweet Yeshua, *todah raba. Todah raba.*

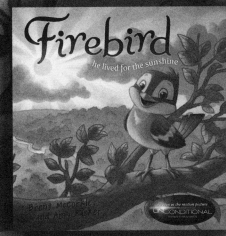